INFILTRATION

INFILTRATION

ANIMUS™ BOOK EIGHT

JOSHUA ANDERLE

MICHAEL ANDERLE

LMBPN

DISRUPTIVE IMAGINATION

LMBPN Publishing
PMB 196, 2540 South Maryland Pkwy
Las Vegas, NV 89109

First US edition, July 2019
Version 1.01, March 2020
eBook ISBN: 978-1-64202-375-6
Print ISBN: 978-1-64202-376-3

Thanks to the JIT Readers

Jeff Eaton
Nicole Emens
Diane L. Smith
John Ashmore
Dave Hicks
Larry Omans
Kelly O'Donnell

If I've missed anyone, please let me know!

Editor
The Skyhunter Editing Team

To Family, Friends and
Those Who Love
to Read.
May We All Enjoy Grace
to Live the Life We Are
Called.

CHAPTER ONE

Hub 103-Vox—better known simply as Vox—was one of the first cloud cities developed, a beautiful if synthetic-looking city floating among the clouds off the coast of Canada. When the sun began to set, there were very few places that could claim to provide a better sight.

However, it was well past sunset, and Kaiden wasn't concerned with sightseeing. Right now, his focus was on a turret that barred his way and he glanced a little irritably at the infiltrator who should have dealt with it already.

He folded his arms and leaned against the wall. "You know, if this takes you two more minutes, I'll tell everyone. Think about your reputation."

Chiyo looked up from the keyboard of her new device, a source-seek gadget that assisted hackers to connect to specific devices and find a path to their connection point. According to her, it would allow her to better aid the mission as she would be able to connect to one device and potentially turn off any others connected to the same node or station. He was well aware that she knew her stuff and had happily bought it for her before they departed to Vox.

But she had used it several times now, and each time, she'd doodled around inside the system—more like a kid with a new toy than a professional with things to do.

"You do know I'm doing this because you didn't wish to keep crawling," she reminded him as she returned her attention to the screen and continued to type. "Do you want to go back into the vents?"

"Good Lord, no," Kaiden protested and glanced at a small opening in the wall about twenty yards away. "Seriously, I've had my fill of that between gigs and the Animus. We need to find other ways to travel around."

"A good soldier is very skilled in stealth. You should be able to walk around without bringing an entire base down on your head."

"You can't say I haven't done better with that when it comes to Animus missions," he pointed out.

"Why Animus missions specifically? Are you more subtle during your real missions?" she inquired.

"Of course, most of my missions are solo. Give me a few more years, and I might be able to take a battalion on at once, but I know my current limits," he said jokingly.

"I'm always sure to make sure he doesn't kill us off and it's more of a chore than you would think." Chief chuckled and suddenly appeared in the air.

"Get more jokes, light bulb," Kaiden retorted.

"Pot and kettle, buddy," the EI countered and his single eye narrowed.

"Nice of you to make an appearance, Chief," Chiyo greeted. "I wondered where you dipped off to."

"I've been enjoying the show, although it's been a slow start so far." The EI cast a somewhat sarcastic look at the ace.

"I'm trying to make this a quick in and out. We don't exactly want to bring attention to ourselves or our actions here," Kaiden pointed out.

"I wouldn't mind, honestly," the infiltrator commented.

He cocked his head. "Really? You just chastised me for it, and now you want to go loud?"

"That wasn't an invitation," she replied with a sigh. "I'm simply saying that corrupt corporations like these are a particular irritation for me. If our actions could bring attention to their misdeeds, I would prefer it."

"Misdeeds? Like what?"

She stopped typing again and turned slowly to look at her teammate. "I was under the impression that this company operated using underhanded methods. That's why we're here for the data, correct?"

Kaiden shook his head. "Nah, not at all. This was a gig Julio handed to me. The contractor is a rival company on this hub. They simply want to see what they are up to."

"What? This is corporate espionage!" Chiyo hissed and her fists clenched.

"I'm sure I told you that—or hinted, at least," the ace muttered and lowered a hand to remind her to keep her voice down. "By the way, are you sure you don't want everyone to know we're here?"

"You...you didn't tell me that we're here to steal, Kaiden." She growled her annoyance and jabbed a finger into his chest armor.

"Technically, any retrieval mission could be seen as stealing," he reasoned with a shrug. "Besides, we're not on land. Cloud cities roll with their own rules, right? This is basically a sport to them. I'm sure someone at the other company will leak that they have the data at some point and these dolts will return the favor. It might not be terribly civil, but it ain't really bad."

Chiyo shook her head and sighed. "Your way of looking at things is frustrating and baffling at the same time."

Kaiden rolled his eyes behind his visor. "You do know my backstory, right? My moral compass is a roulette wheel at this point."

She returned her attention to the seeker, pressed one button, and the turret around the corner swiveled to face the floor. "We'll discuss this later. Let us finish up asap," she said curtly.

"I'm glad, you're still on board." He drew his rifle and prepared to advance.

The infiltrator deactivated the seeker and placed the device on her belt. "I'm still not happy."

"Fair enough, but remember, I took this mission for your sake." He tossed the comment over his shoulder as he walked forward.

"My sake?" she asked and followed quickly.

"You wanted to go on a mission with me, remember? After not being able to help out with the Ramses situation?" he reminded her.

"So? You would take this mission regardless."

"Are you kidding me? Look at all the security they have in here. Do you think I could have done this without my usual destructive flair? If I did take the gig and didn't bring you, I would probably need to call you to bail me out."

"See, he always has you in mind," Chief quipped.

"Quiet, Chief," she said flatly and left him where he still floated.

"*I miss Kaitō.*" The EI snorted and vanished.

They walked unopposed through the hall for several minutes and she surveyed their surroundings. "They don't seem to have many guards here."

"They rely on mechs and drones, but they are all tethered to the alarms. As long as those don't go off, they simply wait on standby in a pod bay," Kaiden explained.

"You would think they would have a few roaming around for added detection. I could have probably broken in here with the skills I had in first year from what I've seen so far."

"That and the right toys," he noted and glanced at her over his shoulder. "You don't know much about cloud cities, do you?"

"Outside of the mechanisms that allow them to hover in the sky for so long, I didn't think they were any different than a normal metropolis."

"Oh, the city tech might be similar, but the culture and economy are way different," Kaiden stated. "Energy is super-expensive, for example, so even major corps like this one have to preserve power when possible. They might be vulnerable like you said, but they have the added security that almost no one arrives on the hub without every official knowing. If something goes down, the new arrivals are the first to get frisked."

"So what does that mean for us when we're finished?" she inquired cautiously.

"Don't worry about it. Julio made sure we're already registered as departed four hours ago," he informed her.

"He's rather skilled in these kinds of things for a bartender," Chiyo observed.

"Trust me, he has dozens of stories of the time before he settled down." He chuckled and shook his head. "You can also trust me when I say he also takes his pound of flesh for all the set-up he had to do. I'll make less than a third of what I usually do for a mission like this. Don't worry about your cut, though. It'll all go to you."

"That's rather nice of you, but I'm not worried about extra credits," she stated.

"Hey, I'll take it if you're offering, but you deserve your piece." Kaiden approached the end of the hall, slid up to the wall, and prepared to peek around the corner. "As I said, I couldn't do a mission like this without you."

The infiltrator stopped, clasped her hands in front of her, and looked away slightly. "I'm glad I can help, but I wanted you to know that you don't have to—" He interrupted her when he held a hand up. "What's wrong?"

"We're not alone in here, it seems," he said cryptically.

"Guards or personnel?" she inquired.

"It doesn't look like either—more like mercs, actually."

"What?" Kaiden stepped away from the wall so she could take his place. She peered around at six figures in black armor who hacked into a door at the end of the hall. "Any idea who they may be?"

"They don't display any emblem or colors, those are stealth suits," he said thoughtfully. "Mercs and gang members usually want to leave a message, but there are mercs who specialize in infiltration and acquisitions and would wear neutral armor for a job."

"It could also be a hacker cell," Chiyo suggested.

"It could be, but don't you guys usually prefer to work from outside your target?" he asked.

"When we can, but tell me, Kaiden, what have I done during the last three years?"

He looked up a little sheepishly. "Fair point."

The infiltrator smiled and looked around the corner again. "Isn't that our destination as well?" She looked at the ace. "Do you think the contractor called in backup?"

"They would have let us know if that was the case." He opened his messages to make sure he hadn't missed anything from Julio. "There could have been a fallback team, but they would have at least given us a warning and waited twenty-four hours from our starting time."

"Then that puts them here at the behest of someone else," Chiyo whispered and frowned as the door opened and the group entered before it closed behind them. "They went in. What should we do?"

Kaiden held his rifle up, powered it down, and opened the chamber to remove the core and replace it. "Change to non-lethal rounds."

She seemed startled for a moment but recovered quickly, drew her pistol, and changed its power core for an arc generator. "You are learning."

"This might actually work out for us. They could take the fall for us," he remarked.

"That's a good idea," she agreed.

"You think so? You do have the spirit for this work, I must say." He closed the chamber and powered his rifle on. "Ready?"

She activated her pistol. "After you."

Kaiden ran to the door and held his weapon ready while Chiyo approached the console. "Can you get in fast?"

She studied the screen. "It won't take any time at all. They used a burst command, which basically forced the electronic lock open temporarily. Kaitō can clean it up in no time and open it."

"At once, madame." Her fox EI nodded in the console screen before he disappeared.

"I counted six. You?" the ace asked and adjusted his rifle against his shoulder.

The infiltrator nodded. "If we catch them by surprise, we should be able to disable them before they can return fire."

"That's what I think. Chief?"

"What do ya need, partner?"

"Get the battle suite ready," he ordered.

"Time for a game of New Duck Hunt," the EI chirped gleefully.

"Heh, haven't played that since I was a kid. I always did get the high score." He grinned.

"Ready to go, Kaiden," Chiyo informed him.

"Go ahead." He pressed the trigger lightly. "Activate, Chief."

The door began to slide as Kaiden's perception heightened and time seemed to slow. As soon as it had opened slightly, he had located one of the mercs and fired a shot. The plan was to fire quickly down the line so six shots delivered six unconscious mercs. Two of the shots found their mark and almost every muscle of the two targets spasmed from the electric bolt. Their legs gave way, but the other four were all able to dodge. Two simply dropped and rolled and the other two activated some kind of metallic shield that absorbed the blast.

The ace's eyes widened. They shouldn't have been able to react that quickly, especially with the heightened senses and agility the battle suite granted him. Not only that, the firing rate of his rifle was faster than a kinetic bullet unless it was fully charged.

"What the hell?"

"Kaiden!" Chiyo called a warning. His surprise had rendered him almost oblivious to the mercs' counterattack. The two who rolled out of the way had already drawn their weapons and each aimed a sub-machine gun at him. He flung himself to the side, yanked out a shock grenade, and threw it while he ducked to avoid their fire. The ordnance bounced along the floor and erupted on the left side of the room. One of his adversaries was eliminated, but the other still had his metallic shield up and it absorbed the electricity into the center of the protective device. What the hell was that thing?

His adversary pressed a trigger on the device's handle. It lit up with the absorbed electricity and released it at him. The suite closed quickly as he retrieved his shield and activated it. The barrier didn't stop the attack but dulled it slightly. It still hurt like a bastard, though, and forced him to his knees.

"What the hell, Chief?" Kaiden gasped as he shook off the effects and forced himself up despite the pain.

"If you'd been hit with the suite activated, that would have hurt a hell of a lot worse," the EI reminded him. *"Pros and cons, partner."*

"All right, good call," he acknowledged. His three adversaries now launched a sustained volley at his shield. "Chiyo, are you..." He glanced over as the infiltrator dashed past the shield and lobbed two grenades of her own. These were flash grenades that blinded the remaining mercs. She lunged at one who continued to fire at her partner and swept his legs out from under him while she charged her pistol. He fell and she thrust her weapon into his chest and fired to shock him and also managed to crack his armor.

"Damn, someone's been hitting the firefight sims," Chief said with a whistle.

"No kidding." The ace frowned at the other two men who had begun to recover. "Well, I shouldn't waste the opportunity." He vaulted over his shield, holstered his rifle, and drew Debonair.

"I guess we aren't going clean anymore, huh?"

"They haven't given us much choice, have they?" He

aimed at the merc who held the reflection device. His target saw his approach and extended his shield.

"It looks like it can reflect lasers. Go for the legs," the EI shouted.

"Got it." The ace aimed quickly and fired three shots. The first two shattered the armor and the final one burned through the man's leg. The injury drew a loud cry of pain, audible despite the helmet, and he toppled. Kaiden pushed forward as he fell to kick him in the head and cracked the visor with the force of the blow.

He looked up into the barrel of a hand cannon aimed by the final merc and immediately raised Debonair. Before either of them could fire, his adversary was struck by an arc of electricity, dropped his weapon, and stumbled while he flailed to regain his balance. Kaiden crossed the few paces between them and powered his armored fist into the chin area of his opponent's helmet. The man landed hard and shook his head for a moment before he tried to stand. Chiyo stepped forward and kicked him down again. His head lolled to the side and he lay motionless.

"Nice work," Kaiden complimented and spun Debonair around his finger before he slid it back into the holster.

The infiltrator looked around. "I don't think they'll work as a fall group anymore."

He laughed. "Hell no. Even an investigator who skipped four years of classes can tell there was a fight here. Still, they'll be occupied with processing these guys rather than looking for us." He swiped his hands along his armor to clean it as best he could. "We should count ourselves lucky the fight didn't trigger any alarms."

"I try to not rely on luck," she retorted crisply and

hurried to the main terminal. "I uploaded a dead-zone command when I tinkered with the turret earlier. It disables alarms, so unless there was a large explosion, we should be fine."

"Oh… Well, nice work once again."

"Good thing she's looking out for your ass." Chief chuckled.

"Yeah, I'll take my earlier griping back if it's not too late." Kaiden turned his attention to one of the unconscious mercs, knelt beside him, and studied his armor while Chief began to scan. He traced his fingers along a very thin line in the underlay and immediately recognized it as disruption lining. As the name implied, the wiring masked signals and made the wearer almost invisible to cameras and other detectors. "Man, if it weren't for the strength of the plating and the disruption lining, I would think this stuff was basic armor—with no accessories and no mods, this stuff is frugal."

"There are mods, but not in the armor," the EI informed him.

"Do what? Are they in the weapons?"

"They do have a couple in their weapons—an advanced one too—but they have mods in their bodies."

His hand flinched. "In their bodies? They're augs?"

"Yeah. From what I read, they have mods for reflexes and increased mental ability. Although those have always been dubious, the reflex mods would explain how they were able to react so quickly."

"Yeah, these guys are better outfitted than most grunts we deal with," he muttered. He unlocked the merc's helmet it and removed it, then stared at the completely pale, blank face with no hair or eyebrows. Tentatively, he opened the eyelids. The man's eyes were white, either from contacts or cosmetic surgery.

"*Man, that's creepy.*" Chief shuddered and the outlines of his avatar spiked in and out for a moment.

"These guys don't half-ass the untraceable thing, that's for sure," Kaiden stood and looked at Chiyo. "Have you had any luck?"

"I'm in," she stated. "I've found the file."

"Were they going for the same thing?" he asked, his gaze drawn back to the body by the oddness of what he'd found.

"No. That's what's strange. It doesn't look like they were downloading anything. They were uploading something," she informed him.

"Uploading? A virus?" he inquired.

"Kaitō is taking a look while I get the data." she looked away from the terminal. "But it was only partially uploaded, so whatever we find won't be completed."

"Unless…" His thought trailed off as he walked over to one of the mercs he'd managed to shoot at the beginning of the fight. He knelt, frisked both bodies, and located a small drive on the second one. The device was triangular and didn't look like it would fit in any slot that he knew of. He paused in his examination and looked at the helmet. While he wanted to simply have Chief scan it, he was too curious for his own good.

He unlocked the helmet and hauled it off, and sure enough, it had obscured the same featureless head but with one major exception. This one had a device implanted along the side of his skull—a neurotech, he realized, someone with augmentations that allow them to interface with technology. The principle was similar to the technician's suite but way riskier as they needed a special EI to use it without frying their minds and even then, it wasn't a guarantee. He moved the head around and peered a little more closely. This one had considerable work done.

Kaiden stood and stepped beside Chiyo. "Do you think you can use this?"

She glanced at the device. "That's a—" Her words failed as she recoiled and stared at the body behind her in surprise. She was clearly unnerved but after a moment, she turned back to the terminal and continued her work. "I've completed this. Let me shut it down and clean up."

"Good, we can finish here and be back in Seattle in no —" He spun at a sharp, ominous click. One of the mercs had come round, found his feet, and now aimed his gauntlet at them. "Dammit!" The ace grabbed his partner and hurled them both aside as their adversary fired a missile at them. The attack struck the terminal and exploded. Almost immediately, an alarm sounded. The infiltrator drew her pistol and fired successfully at the assailant. He stiffened as the shock struck home before he simply sagged, rolled over, and passed out again.

"It looks like that was enough of an explosion to trigger the alarms." Kaiden huffed irritably as he stood and offered a hand to his teammate.

"I can't use the terminal to turn it off now." She gestured at the wrecked machine. "Obviously."

"Then, let's make our exit, darlin'," he declared, hefted his rifle, and rushed out of the room with her close behind.

CHAPTER THREE

Kaiden slid along the ground and aimed at a reactivated turret that currently tried its damnedest to fry him. He fired Sire but had yet to change the core so delivered a bolt of electricity instead of plasma. It was enough to stun the weapon and he scrambled to his feet and drew Debonair to finish the job.

"So, are all the turrets online now?" he asked as he powered his rifle down and opened it to exchange the cores.

"Most were reset when the alarm went off," Chiyo confirmed. "I still have control of the cameras, but without access to a central terminal, I won't be able to keep them offline for much longer."

"We spent all this time and effort to come in stealthily and it goes up in smoke because of some ghoulish-looking idiot's missile," he muttered and snapped his rifle closed. A thunderous clanking sound indicated the rapid approach of a group of droids—Soldier or Assault units, probably.

He prepared for the inevitable fight. "Do you think you can find out what we'll have to deal with as we make our escape?"

She readied her sub-machine gun and stood beside him. "From the initial look at the inventory and map, they have one thousand and sixty-two droids available in the building."

"And how many of those are combat-ready?" he asked.

"They have one thousand and sixty-two droids available," she repeated.

He sighed when he accepted the obvious interpretation of that. "So, we should try our best to escape instead of taking them all on?"

So you're not worried about points this time?" Chief asked.

"A score isn't that impressive when it's etched on a tombstone," Kaiden replied and began to charge a shot while he leaned closer to his teammate. "Do you have a map?"

"Of course, but all the normal exits are locked down, and my guess is that the defenses in those areas were the first to be reactivated. I suggest we look for a less traditional escape route."

The ace looked behind him to the device on his back. "I have something that could work. But we'll need to find a window or something to bust out of." The mechanical clanking drew closer. "I'll hold that thought for now."

"Make sure you destroy them thoroughly," Chiyo warned. "They shouldn't currently be able to send their camera feedback to a cloud, but they can still record the footage to their own internal devices. If you don't want anyone to know we were here—"

"You know you don't have to worry about that," he chided playfully as the first few droids trundled around the corner. "Firing." He released the trigger, the blast aimed immediately in front of the group. It exploded on contact and launched six droids to spiral into a clumsy heap.

Chiyo began to fire as he ran closer to the defenders. He counted fifteen in total in this wave. They were well-armored but were designed to withstand kinetic rounds. Two of those that were caught in his initial fire were now upright. He fired Sire in quick shots to eliminate three more. He jumped back as their opponents retaliated and managed a few shots as he retrieved a shock grenade. A mechanical broke from the group and dashed forward as a blade popped out of its arm. It managed only a few steps before it was felled by a barrage from the infiltrator.

Kaiden hurled the grenade, vented his rifle, and backed away to avoid being caught in the explosion. The shock erupted and blanketed the droids in a field of electricity, but he frowned when this barely slowed the assault. He didn't know if it was a dampener field he hadn't picked up or a new upgrade, but it would appear he would need to rethink his gear going forward. The electrical weaponry seemed to have lost some of its effectiveness—a real pity, considering they were way cheaper to replace than thermal or nano grenades.

The ace held Sire up with one hand and drew Debonair with the other to target two of the remaining droids. One fell without much resistance. The other, however, was quite stubborn, continued to stand through the barrage, and returned fire. Kaiden was able to sidestep a couple of blasts, but one caught him in the shoulder. A metallic crack indicated that his armor had shattered and although the pain was dulled, it was enough for him to flinch and drop the pistol. The loss was annoying but not disastrous as Sire had cooled enough by now.

He slammed the vent closed and charged a shot. The two recovering droids had found their feet and joined the other tenacious attackers. He darted to the side and backpedaled away from the laser fire. The mechanicals pushed closer together for better aim as he retreated, exactly as he'd hoped they would. He spun quickly and pulled the trigger to deliver a strike to the droid in the middle. It was completely destroyed when it was enveloped in the blast, and the other two, already compromised, simply melted into ungainly heaps of metal from the residual energy of the explosion.

Kaiden stood and walked to where he'd dropped Debonair while Chiyo eliminated the last of the droids. He retrieved his weapon and checked it for damage, then studied the defeated robotic mob. Of the fifteen, it looked like he'd accounted for nine in total? Maybe ten, but one of them had sustained damage from both his and Chiyo's weapons, so call it a split.

"Not bad for an infiltrator," he commented as she walked over. Her sub-machine gun folded into itself as she put it away. "I also noticed the moves you displayed back in the terminal room. Have you put in some work?"

"Steadily, yes." She nodded and surveyed the wreckage. "I am at Nexus to further my hacking abilities and technological knowledge, but I know those are only two of the obligations of my class. I need to work on my stealth capabilities and my fighting skills in particular."

"The fruits of your labor are certainly showin'," he complimented. "You claimed a fair number of those."

"I'm glad I could help, although if I may point something out…" She folded her arms and looked at his shoulder. "I might not have equaled your droid kill-count, but my armor is still intact."

"That's because I was the more attractive target." He chuckled and holstered Debonair. "In a metaphorical sense, but if you choose to take that as literal, then thank you kindly."

Chiyo shook her head, but he heard her laugh quietly over the comms. She looked at her weapon. "I don't think I would have done as well without this. Thank you for providing it."

"It's actually from Julio's personal collection," he admitted. "You'll have to return it along with all the gear when we get back. If you like it enough you can try to buy it off him, but you should prepare to haggle. On the last gig, some of the others wanted to keep their stuff, and the prices he threw out were insane."

She shrugged. "It is nice, but I'll let him keep it, for now. I don't know when I'll do another one of these." She peered down the hall when they heard another wave approach. "Assuming we get out of here first, of course. You said you had an idea?"

Kaiden nodded. "Yeah, but we need an exit point—preferably a window or fire exit or something that leads to the side of the building."

"There is a line of windows down the hall," she said and pointed to the west. "But from that position, considering where the building is located, we would effectively jump off the edge of the station itself."

"That's perfect, actually." He nodded and a green dot flared on his map. "Come on."

When the duo reached the expanse of windows, they were locked down by metal panels. Kaiden gestured at the infiltrator to open them and she retrieved the seeker device. "I can open one at a time for a brief period. That should be enough, correct?"

"Yep, but be prepared to jump." He nodded, took a few steps back, and readied himself to leap through the window.

"You have absorption mods in your armor or maybe a parachute?" she asked as she activated the override and the defensive panel began to retract.

"Of a sort, but we won't float down to earth, That would take too long anyway."

Chiyo sighed as she put the device away. "Do you have to be so cryptic?"

"I suppose not." More clangs and thumps confirmed the presence of droids close behind them. "But do you want to wait around for an explanation?" he asked and extended a hand.

She shook her head and took hold. He rushed toward the window when enough of the glass was exposed. The two crashed through into a free-fall in the night sky, miles above the Earth. He activated the skyhook device on his back. A wire launched from the top of the device and a large balloon expanded rapidly from the tip. He pulled Chiyo in closer as their dropship flew in from above, snagged the line, and hauled them in.

It took only seconds. He blinked in the air, and in the next moment, they were in the passenger bay of the dropship. "Neat trick," his partner said, and he released her as she slowly pulled away.

"Yeah, I'm glad it worked out," Kaiden admitted and flopped onto the bench behind him.

"You weren't sure?"

"It's the first time I've used it," he admitted. "Another of Julio's suggestions. He said I should have one since we were going to a cloud city. I half-suspected that he simply wanted to make me buy something off him, but I have to admit it's rather handy."

She sat on the opposite bench, removed her helmet, and her hair tumbled out as she placed the headgear down beside her. "You really couldn't have simply found a mission where you needed me to shut down some trip lasers or something?"

He took his helmet off and smiled. "You know that wouldn't have been much fun."

"*Hey, wanna take the wheel, buddy? I ain't getting paid to chauffer,*" Chief chided.

The ace stood and rolled his shoulders as he made his way to the cockpit. "Yeah, yeah, hold your—" He paused for a moment as the door to the cockpit opened. "Wait, you aren't getting paid at all."

"*That's what's bothering you?*" The EI chuckled. The two

began to bicker as the door shut behind him. Chiyo exhaled a deep breath and stretched out. She did have to admit it probably wouldn't have been as much fun.

Maybe a little more relaxing, though.

Detective D'Arcy studied the crime scene, and Lord, it was a mess. There were six bodies—if one could call them that—a heap of droid pieces a few halls down, and a destroyed terminal that was quite important to the company. Sections of wall and flooring had either exploded or melted, or were damaged in a variety of ways, and so far, no video or audio evidence could be found.

Mondays were a hell of a drag.

He continued his morose survey as other officers and Lexsys Corporation's personnel security combed the room. A few of their technicians tried to salvage what they could from the terminal's remains. Apparently, it didn't have a standard backup as it was isolated from the main server room for a particular reason. Of course, they made it a point to ensure that he wasn't privy to that reason.

A forensics officer approached one of the gory remains and the detective walked across and knelt beside him. The man scooped some of the evidence into a vial. "It looks pretty gruesome," he muttered.

JOSHUA ANDERLE & MICHAEL ANDERLE

"Right?" The technician sighed. "I know these corporate games are par for the course, but they are usually civil enough with each other." He gestured to the dark muck inside the empty armor. "What were the other guys carrying that turned them into this?"

Dario walked into Merrick's office and placed a cup of black tea on the desk. The leader studied the report and didn't appear to be happy at all. He wasn't angry or depressed, but something had not gone as planned.

"Care to talk about it?" Dario asked, sat on the edge of the massive desk, and sipped from his own cup. "We have several teams out and about right now. Which one messed up?"

"The Lexsys team," Merrick responded flatly. He looped his fingers through the handle of the teacup and brought it gingerly to his lips. He held it there without actually taking a sip. "They weren't able to upload the spyware and tampering virus."

"Really, now? And after all that money we paid for specialized golems," the other man grumbled before he casually took another sip. "I guess we can go back to the synthetic drawing board and fiddle around with the next batch. What took them out?"

"Kaiden Jericho."

Dario stopped the cup midway to his lips and turned his head slowly to face the boss. "Really, now? How is it that he interferes with our work when we aren't even targeting him anymore?"

"It appears he was on a mission for the rival company, Strato. It was coincidental."

"But still annoying—and it's also a hell of a coincidence."

"I agree," Merrick replied and finally took a sip before he placed the cup back on the table. "I'll have to look into how he got the mission. Maybe there is an informant somewhere along the way. I'll have a team look into Strato and send someone to investigate the dealer."

"We have the resources for now, certainly, but I think we'll need to make a decision regarding our former priority target," the assistant suggested.

"Kaiden was always merely a potential feather in our cap. The priority was always the EI," his superior corrected and pushed the tablet forward so he could lean an elbow on the desk. "But if he continues to get in the way, we'll have to make him a priority elimination."

"You have my contact info. Let me know," Dario offered.

"I have a different job for you, but it may intersect with this matter." The man slid the tablet closer to Dario, who picked it up to see a picture of Kaiden and another student behind him.

"Who is this?" he asked and zoomed in on the female accomplice.

"Chiyo Kana, daughter of Gendo Orikasa."

His face assumed an expression of surprise and amusement as he looked at the picture once again. "She certainly took a different direction than a child of a zaibatsu leader would normally take, didn't she?"

Merrick leaned his head into his open palm and tapped

his desk with the fingers of his other hand. "There seems to be some friction between father and daughter in this case. However, I'm concerned about the repercussions of her involvement."

"How so?"

"She's a skilled technician—a top-tier infiltrator according to her file. If she recovered the drive from the neurotech golem and decided to look into it, she'll see the programs and commands installed into the device."

"Are you worried she would use them against us? Or maybe that it would lead back to us?" Dario inquired.

"We developed each suite in preparation to attack specific security systems. The security that defended the Lexsys OS was designed by Gendo's company," the leader explained.

"Ah, I see." He finished his tea, placed the cup on the desk, and stood. "You're worried she'll connect the dots and tell her father."

"Correct." Merrick nodded. "While I doubt even she could trace it back to us—or anyone she might have connections to—I'm sure a program that specifically countered something developed by her father would cause her concern. She will notify Gendo, and he'll begin looking into it."

"And with his vast network and the technology at his disposal, he will begin a manhunt that could lead him to our doorstep," the assistant surmised.

"Eventually, perhaps, but he will certainly be on high alert, and we have yet to establish a foothold in the Mirai Zaibatsu." The leader took the tablet back and opened a file. "So far, we have taken control of half of the companies we have targeted, but Mirai is an important piece."

"Having control over a zaibatsu with nearly a dozen companies in its thrall is very enticing. But with the companies we do have and the others we're looking to amass, shouldn't it be more like a cherry on top of our plans rather than a primary ingredient? Mirai and the companies attached to it all focus on technological and security development. Surely with the other corporations we have at our disposal, all we need is to acquire their schematics and reverse-engineer anything we would need from them."

"That's the fallback plan, yes," Merrick agreed. "But they constantly improve and always create something new. More importantly, having access to them would allow us a stronger foothold in both the region and in our preparations."

"Oh, good, you are still thinking about that," Dario said happily. "I began to wonder if I was the only one who cared anymore, considering how much sneaking around we've done."

"There is much to be done, Dario. We can't simply storm in ill-prepared," his superior chastised. "Even if the mission is successful, we will have to deal with the fallout, which means our plan will no doubt lead to a war we will have to face along with the war we fear is coming."

"I'm aware of that, boss." The assistant sighed although his smile didn't falter. "We're doing all this not because we need it to take the Academy, but because taking the Academy is the first step to taking the WC and then preparing for the inevitable—all that doom and gloom." He looked up at the Arbiter Organization's leader and shrugged. "I simply think we need to enjoy ourselves a little more. Everything has been so tense lately and we need to relieve some stress from time to time. What's the point of surviving an apocalypse if we're all Sad Sacks by the end of it."

Merrick, despite his anxiety, chuckled briefly. "I do wish I could have your temperament, even for a few minutes," he confessed. "I'll leave the Mirai mission to you from here on. I had hoped we could do this through simple business and trickery, but it appears it may need a personal touch."

"Which I'll be happy to provide—" Dario's eyes lit up, and he snapped his fingers. "Oh right, you said this mission might cross with our Kaiden problem."

"Potentially. If Chiyo is close enough with Kaiden that she would accompany him on a mission, I would assume that if she brings herself into this, she will bring him in as well."

"And that means I'll finally have an opportunity to meet the boy," the other man responded cheerfully. "I wonder if I should bring that assassin woman with me—the one I recruited from the EX-10."

"As I said, I'll leave the mission to you." Merrick opened a holoscreen and began to work. "I simply request two things."

"Of course, request away."

"One, drop past the R and D department. They will provide you with a device that will assist in the fallback option," he explained. "And secondly..." He looked up from his screen. "Do what you see fit, but please leave Gendo alive for now."

"I don't see a need to kill him. Not yet anyway."

"Even still, I know it seems to be a preference for you to eliminate problems rather than find workarounds. But keeping the head of the zaibatsu alive is important for now. That aside, the golems aren't advanced enough yet to replicate specific people, so it would cause an unnecessary commotion if he were killed or suddenly disappeared."

"I'll keep a hand tied," Dario promised and moved to leave as the doors to the room opened automatically. "One way or another, we'll have the help of the Mirai soon enough." With that, he waved behind him as the door closed.

"We certainly will now," Merrick whispered and allowed himself a confident smile.

CHAPTER FIVE

The sound of an emergency siren blared into Kaiden's sleeping mind although he didn't react with surprise or shock, only irritation as he went to smack his alarm. The instinctive response was unfortunate since it was Chief who actually made the sound.

"Ow, dammit…" he muttered and rubbed his temple.

"You gotta think fast, even first thing in the mornin.'" The EI chuckled.

"You can also choose less annoying sounds to wake me up with," he complained as he slid out of his bed and stretched.

"Look, we tried that chirping bird and gentle singing nonsense. It doesn't get you moving. It's all or nothing when it comes to waking your ass up," Chief countered.

He made no comment. This was the first day of the week and he'd only had about five hours of sleep after he'd returned from the gig. He moved his tired body to his dresser and located an Academy shirt and pants before he headed to the shower. It had taken a couple of years, but he finally began to feel everything catch up to him in the early morning. All the pain, fatigue, and general moroseness. Maybe he needed to start drinking tea or something.

As he shuffled down the hall and tried to keep his eyelids half-closed to block the sunlight creeping through the windows, he wondered how Chiyo fared after her first merc gig. Or, at least, what he assumed was her first gig.

Well, he would find out soon enough.

He placed his tray of breakfast on the usual table, picked his fork up, and spun it for a moment. It shouldn't be long before Chiyo arrived.

"Hello, friend Kaiden!" He turned and waved at a cheerful Genos. He wasn't whom he'd expected to arrive first, but he wouldn't complain.

"Morning, Genos—no food?" he questioned as the Tsuna took a seat.

"No, we eat at the Tsuna dorms, remember?"

"Yeah, that's right," Kaiden agreed and scratched his head. "You would think they would start integrating mealtimes. Eating and chatting together builds camaraderie like crazy."

"Kin Jaxon stated that it is something they discuss in alliance meetings, but considering our specific diets, it would require moving everything from the dorms to the cafeteria and making sure to increase supply in case the human students want anything," the mechanist explained.

"I doubt many would be so brave as to try Tsuna delicacies, but the nice fruits and seafood you guys get might spark some interest." He took a bite of bacon. "You said that Jaxon got this from an alliance meeting? Tsuna and human alliance or something?"

Genos nodded. "Indeed, most meetings are called by each individual party as they think of ideas for better relations, then they come together and debate."

"I'm surprised you don't take part. You seem interested in better relations and all that." He pointed a fork at the alien. "After all, the only reason we really started getting to know each other is because you spoke up. I was kind of dumbfounded at meeting an alien for the first time."

"To be fair, my people are more accustomed to it in general, considering our history," his companion replied. "I am happy that I have been able to make such fast friends, but I haven't traveled much outside our circle and especially since the new arrivals have come in."

"Have you played chaperone?" Kaiden asked.

"To an extent. I pass my knowledge on and explain how best to interact with humans," he replied.

"That's had to lead to some interesting results." The ace snickered.

"How so?" Genos asked and tapped his infuser. Kaiden darted his gaze away and took a sip of juice.

"Good morning, Kaiden, Genos." Chiyo greeted them with a wan smile.

"Greetings, friend Chiyo." The Tsuna reciprocated with a wave as the infiltrator took a seat and placed her tablet on top of the table.

"Howdy, Chi, how are you this— Are you all right?" The ace frowned when he noticed the haggard appearance of the generally alert and immaculate young woman.

"I didn't get much sleep," she admitted and fumbled for her coffee.

"*None at all, actually,*" Kaitō informed them from the tablet screen. "*Madame was up all night researching that drive you recovered.*"

"The one the neurotech had?" he inquired. "Thanks, but I was only curious. You didn't have to—"

She held a hand up to stop him as she took a long drink of coffee, then set the cup down gently. "I was equally as curious. I hadn't planned to spend more than an hour or two looking into it, but I found something troubling."

He leaned against the table. "And what was that?"

The infiltrator raised two fingers. "A couple of things. One was the fact that they tried to upload market data from the contractor's company into Lexsys' systems."

"So they were hired by them, then." Kaiden sighed and took a swig of his drink.

"I don't think so. I would think they would simply hand the data in or send it remotely if that was the case. They wanted this to be unnoticed."

"You ran into another merc group?" Genos asked and the ace shrugged.

"As best I can tell, their gear and equipment were far too sophisticated for them to simply be gang members or jobbers," he theorized. "It could have been another private group, maybe, but they had no symbols and no real features to potentially identify them on a database."

"That sounds odd," the alien remarked.

He laughed. "You're telling me. They looked creepier with the helmets off."

"That actually brings me to my next point," Chiyo

continued and her companions returned their attention to her. "I found the program they used to hack in, and it was created to bypass a specific security system."

"That sounds par for the course," he commented.

"Normally, yes. On simple security, all it takes is the right program to deactivate it. But what troubled me is that the security system on the Lexsys mainframe was a Mirai-developed suite only released four weeks ago and updated three days ago."

"Mirai?" Kaiden frowned. The name sounded familiar. After a moment's thought, he snapped his fingers in realization. "That's—"

"That's your father's company, correct?" Genos finished and the ace let his hand fall into his lap.

"Yes, and their system is something that cannot simply be overwritten like that," Chiyo said, her voice low and troubled. "Not normally, anyway. They are leaders in the field. Even with my knowledge of their codes and tools, I have difficulty finding exploits or gaining access to anything they protect. And their latest upgrade..." She trailed off, her eyes narrowed in thought.

"Do you regularly hack into your old man's stuff?" Kaiden asked and finished his juice.

"Old habits, I suppose. Plus, I still have associates I am fond of who work in his employ. I like to help them when I can," she stated.

"Did you inform your father of this?" the Tsuna asked.

"I sent a message, but I don't know if it's reached him yet. He may already be aware."

"Some kind of back-door measure that sends a signal to alert them if their system has been bypassed?" the ace asked, and both his friends looked at him in surprise. "I can talk tech to some extent." He looked over at the R and D building. "Between talks with Chiyo and Laurie, I've picked up a few tidbits."

"Also me," Chief remarked and was met with silence.

"That could be one way, yes," Chiyo agreed. "However, I found other targets on the drive. Other companies that have recently been bought up or merged with another in the last few months."

"That's probably not a coincidence." Genos reasoned.

"It ties back to the data they were uploading at Lexsys." She nodded. "Using that info, Lexsys could have been several steps ahead of Stratos, which would eventually lead to a great financial loss for them and a large boon for Lexsys and finally, Stratos' downfall or perhaps a buyout like the others."

"So it's some white collar crime stuff?" Kaiden speared a breakfast sausage with his fork. "I'm sure that's interesting to someone."

"You should take a look at the companies," she suggested. "They are all in different fields—robotics, military arms, medical—but they are all being bought up by the same companies."

"Isn't that how these places operate?" he asked. "Everyone is trying to be a megacorp these days."

"Indeed, but to have it happen in such a domino effect is concerning, and to be in the middle of it—"

"Hey, we don't have to do jack," the ace protested. "We did our work and simply happened to stumble into this mess."

Chiyo looked at him for a long moment. She was obviously tired, but there was concern in her eyes. "I know, maybe I'm paranoid. But I believe that something will happen and that my fath—that Mirai will be swept up in it."

Kaiden finished his sausage and nodded slowly. He reached out and took the drive. "I get it now. You're looking out for your old stomping grounds." He took his plate of pancakes and placed it on her tray. "Eat up, and maybe think about taking the day off and playing catch-up later. You look exhausted."

"Where are you going?" she asked.

"I'm gonna have Laurie look into this. If anyone knows about this sort of thing, he's the best I can think of," he answered as he tossed his trash and set the tray on top of the can. "I'll catch up with you later."

His companions watched him walk away before Genos turned to Chiyo. "I can't tell if this situation is fortuitous or not."

She sighed, took her knife and fork, and cut into the pancakes. "I suppose that all depends on how it plays out."

CHAPTER SIX

"You can't barge—" A guard stammered a protest as Kaiden let himself into Laurie's office.

"Hey, Prof. Are you here?" he called and the man spun in his chair.

"Ah, dear Kaiden. Good to see you." The professor gestured cheerfully at the guard who tried to pull his visitor away. "It's all right, George. He's on the list."

"Uh...right, sir. Sorry, I didn't think any students were allowed in here." He apologized quickly and released Kaiden's shirt.

"They aren't, but he's the exception," Laurie stated.

"My name is Kaiden Jericho," the ace informed him. "Keep it in mind."

"Yeah, all right." He nodded and left the room.

"Are you doing all right, Kaiden? Do you have another issue with Chief?" his host questioned as Kaiden took a seat.

"Nothing like that this time, thankfully." He placed the

drive on the table and slid it across. "Actually, I wanted you to look into something."

The man picked the drive up and examined it closely. "This is a neurotech drive." He placed it on a panel that began to scan it and turned to his monitor screen. "Where did you get this?"

"Out on gig. I ran into a group of mercs while in the Lexsys HQ," he explained.

"You were in Vox? Beautiful city, isn't it? It launched on my tenth birthday," Laurie stated merrily. "Although what were you doing at Lexsys? Nothing unreasonable, I assume?"

"Do you think that everyone who comes here will lead lives of sunshine and gumdrops, Prof?" he asked.

"So I'd rather not know, then?"

Kaiden rubbed the back of his neck. "I doubt you'd be liable in any way, but the rules up there are so screwy, it's probably best not to mention it."

"Agreed. Back to this drive." The professor looked at him. "What I see is rather troubling."

"You broke in that quickly?" he asked, astonished despite his knowledge of the man's skill.

"Technically, Aurora did, but I did create her so I can take some credit." He looked at the screen again. "Files, security counters…there are several things here."

"Yeah. Chiyo took a look and told me about all that."

"I had hoped that you would refrain from dragging your friends into your misadventures," Laurie said wearily.

"Hey, it was her idea. Well…kind of," he retorted.

"I see." He leaned back and folded his arms. "Tell me, Kaiden, what do you know of neurotechs?"

"Not a lot more than the basic stuff most people would know, I think," he confessed and tipped his chair back as he shifted into a more comfortable position. "They're augs who have a special device in their heads which uses a mixture of chemicals, mods, and augmentations to allow them to interface with technology in different ways. It's like the technician's suite."

"Our suite is much more complex and powerful than anything like that, I can assure you." The man huffed with a trace of indignation.

"Are you getting territorial now?" He chuckled.

"I'm only correcting misinformation," Laurie assured him. "But do you know the repercussions of such a condition?"

"Yeah...at best, you deal with migraines and hallucinations. At worst, it can lead to catatonia or..." He thought back to the creature in Dallas from years before, flinched involuntarily, and almost toppled. When he'd stabilized himself, he looked up. "You can become a neurosik."

"Indeed, but there is a state in between, one that isn't talked about much because we know so little about it —paratechs."

"They spontaneously jump out of ships?" Kaiden asked humorously, although this only caused the professor to rub his temples.

"It is an amalgam of parasite and tech, smartass." The man huffed. "It is when a neurotech's augmentions turn against him and reduce him to a vegetative state, but not so braindead that he can't be exploited."

"Exploited? How?" Kaiden leaned forward and glanced cautiously at the drive.

"By installing the right software into a neurotech's mental augmentation, they can be pupated as if they were a droid," Laurie explained.

The ace's lip curled as he recoiled instinctively from the device. "That sounds creepy. I'm not afraid of death, but having someone control me like that? Seriously, it gives me chills." He shuddered and focused on the professor. "Do you think this guy was one of those paratechs?"

"Looking at one of these programs, it seems likely. Not only that, but it could link up to control others."

"Wait, what? I didn't look at all the mercs, but he was the only one I saw with a device like that."

"The others wouldn't need something like that, only an antenna augmentation in their brain or along the top part of their spine." He motioned to the positions with his hand.

"You mean like my implant?" Kaiden asked with a sudden tremor of nervousness.

"And again, you compare my work with common appliances," the professor muttered.

"Stuff like that is common?"

"In certain circles, yes." He nodded vigorously.

He shook his head. "Those guys looked weird enough without being all hive-mind. It really completes the zombie look."

"Zombie?" Laurie questioned.

"They were all featureless—no pupils or hair, thin skin, and moved like nothing I've seen outside the Animus. They had augs and mods, but maybe that link let them move so inhumanly because they weren't controlling their own bodies," he surmised.

The other man was silent. Golems. What the student

had described were golems—the very same type they used in Project Orson. His lips pursed as he reached slowly to his console and pressed a button. Chief appeared in the screen, surprise evident as his eye bulged. He quickly began to type a message to the EI.

The door to the room opened and Cyra entered. "Hey, Professor, do you have—oh, hey. You're that Kaiden kid."

"Not a kid, but close." He stood and offered a hand. "Chiyo's told me about you. She thinks very highly of your skills."

"And I think the same," she replied with a smile and shook his hand. "It's nice to finally meet you. So you're here for a little chat with the professor."

"I learn something new anytime I'm here, whether I like it or not." He looked at the other man. "He seems to have gone quiet now, though."

"Cyra, take this." Laurie tossed the drive to her. She released Kaiden's hand quickly and caught it but almost dropped it in surprise.

"What's this?"

"A neurotech drive. Take it to research and look into it for me, would you?" he requested.

"Do you think you can find something else? You seemed to have it all figured out rather quickly," the ace commented.

There might be more to learn from the drive but in reality, Laurie wanted her to leave. He needed some alone time with Kaiden. Well, with one exception.

"And please contact Sasha and tell him to get here as soon as he can."

Cyra nodded, holding the drive close. "Um...all right,

I'll get right on it, sir." She left the room quickly and the ace turned to face him.

"I can't say I've ever seen you so direct, what's up?" he asked and sat again.

The professor sighed and turned his monitor. Kaiden frowned when he saw Chief inside. "What the— When did you leave?"

"I had a pushy invite," the EI stated and his color changed to a worried blue. *"Listen, partner. I had a quick chat with the professor, and there's something we have to talk about."*

"And that is?" He felt a sense of unease from these two —a rather unnerving combination, considering who they were.

Chief looked at the professor to see if he would speak. "You were the one who wanted to break it to him," Laurie pointed out.

"In bits and pieces. There's too much to tell him all at once, don't ya think?" Chief replied.

Kaiden began to feel rather irate. "You both know I'm not a fan of secrets, especially with this EI stuff, and that's what this sounds like."

"Yeah, in a way, but also other stuff," Chief admitted. He looked down for a moment, then back up. *"Do you remember that pirate station test? How the captain spoke gibberish about who you were and all that?"*

"Yeah? What about it?"

"And do you remember that crashed team you saw at the beginning of the Adva final? The one that was happy you 'made it?'" he continued.

"Again, yes." The ace clenched his teeth in frustration. "Where are you taking this?"

"And remember how you said I looked more real?"

He was silent this time, and while he hadn't connected the dots yet, he was certain about one thing. "I won't like this, will I?"

"It depends on your point of view, really." Chief's eye closed and then opened again. Kaiden saw himself in half of his view like he was looking at himself from the monitor screen.

"I guess I should say our point of view," Chief stated.

CHAPTER SEVEN

A man stood at the top floor of an immensely tall building in Tokyo and gazed out across the cityscape. He didn't actually take in the view or look for anything specific but merely stared out as he remained motionless and deep in thought. It was all simply visual white noise.

Someone had targeted him. That was nothing new, really. If you had money and power, you became a target. There was no handbook for this kind of thing, but there were common rules you learned along the way. He learned this at a very young age, something that was both fortunate for his understanding and unfortunate for his reality.

He drew in a deep breath. Another spy was caught, but his men were not able to find anything of note and when the police took him away, all they could charge him with was trespassing and attempted robbery. But he hadn't simply tried to steal an expensive piece of equipment. If that was his only goal, he could have honestly tried to take one of the ornate figures decorating the lobby. They were much smaller and even if he sold it on the lower end, he could have paid six months' rent with only one of those.

Instead, the intruder was found on the fourth floor where he tried to gain entry to one of the lead technicians' office. He was plainly dressed in a brown jacket and blue jeans with no distinguishing features. But he had seen something in the trespasser's eyes—or, rather, a lack of something like he merely stared into a void.

The door to his office opened. "Sir, are you still here?" his assistant asked.

"Of course, Rei," he replied and turned to head to his desk chair. "It seems I've spent most of my life in my office now. I haven't felt like that since I was young."

"It's probably for the best right now, Gendo, sir," she stated and approached the desk. "Considering the circumstances, we don't know if someone is trying to make a move that could put you in jeopardy."

"I doubt this incident is the first step into a kidnapping or assassination plot." He sighed, picked up a vape pen, and took a slow drag. "Is there something that needs my attention?"

"We received a message from your dau—from Chiyo, sir," she stated and handed him the tablet.

"We're alone. Call her what she is." He let the vapor trail from his mouth as he took the tablet. "Maybe if I had thought that way, I would hear from her more often."

The assistant was at a loss for words. "I'm...sorry, sir."

Gendo was silent as he focused on the message and his eyes widened slowly the more he read. "This is... Someone was able to make an override command for our new security system?"

"I can have the team look into it right away, but I wanted you to know first."

He placed the tablet on his desk, linked his fingers together, and thought about it. "Have them look into it immediately. I need to send a message of my own."

Sasha walked briskly into Laurie's office. "Cyra called me. It's rather odd of you to not invite me your—" He saw Kaiden seated in a chair across from the professor with his head down, his back tense and one leg bobbing, and his hands gripped on the sides of his chair. He looked a mixture of confused and furious. That was not a great combination, especially for him.

The commander's walk slowed, and he looked from Kaiden to Laurie, who had a grim expression on his face. That simple fact was equally troubling. He also noticed Chief's avatar in the screen of the monitor.

"I believe I might have some idea of what is going on, but do you care to elaborate, Laurie?" he asked and gave the other man an expectant look.

"He knows now, Sasha," the professor stated. It was a cryptic reply, but he understood in an instant.

He walked over slowly and placed a hand on the ace's back. "Kaiden, I know you must be troubled, but believe me, we didn't want to keep this a secret after everything that happened."

"I know." Kaiden's reply was quick, monotone, and curt at first. The commander couldn't tell if he was angry or too busy thinking things over to manage more than that, but he continued. "Chief explained to me…well, the whole thing. I guess, all in all, it didn't require much, but I kind of wish he was a little more thorough. Like about the part where I was a guinea pig for some WC project that had me going around and taking care of their problems. Maybe it was cheaper than hiring someone?"

For once, Sasha wasn't sure of what to say at this point. It didn't help that he couldn't gauge Kaiden's feelings at the moment. The ace held a hand up. "Before you say anything, yeah. I get that I wasn't actually 'really' there. It was those golem things. Some sort of skin suit, like the things I faced yesterday."

"Yesterday?" Sasha looked at Laurie.

"He did a mercenary gig and ran into a team of golems —ones I suspect to be from AO considering the modifications he told me about," Laurie explained.

"Right. Those guys, who may or may not be after me but definitely the school." Kaiden leaned back and Sasha was somewhat startled by how nonchalant the look on his face was. "A secret club filled with elite members, maybe, who are looking to take over the world or force society to conform to them. Perhaps, but who knows?" He rolled his eyes. "Laurie said you guys don't really know much yet, so I guess I can look forward to dealing with that someday."

"We aren't sure of anything regarding them, Kaiden," Sasha said and dragged in a deep breath. "This is the most active they have ever been, but we still aren't sure of their overall intentions. To most, they are basically a modern Illuminati. Most believe them to be a myth or merely a failed society from decades ago. We aren't sure what their aims are."

"And if they try to make a move against the Academy, we and the WC will handle it," Laurie promised.

"Helpful," Kaiden chided and let his arms hang loosely at his sides. "It doesn't explain why they sent those Asiton robots after me in the Animus."

Laurie really had told him everything, hadn't he? He arrived only fifteen minutes after he had received the message. Cyra was no slouch and he was sure she had sent the message almost immediately after Laurie had requested it. He realized that he wasn't there to help inform Kaiden but to play damage control. He crossed behind the ace and pulled out the other chair, sat slowly, and balled his fists together. It wouldn't do to force him to say anything. That might simply anger him. Instead, he waited for him to ask a question. He also didn't want to rush in and repeat everything again since he didn't know what he'd already been told. That might anger him as well.

"By the way, Commander, did you know I'm a cyborg now?" Sasha looked up in surprise. Kaiden tilted his head slightly to reveal a faint yellow glow in his left eye. "Weird, ain't it? I bet even you didn't think something like this would happen back when we first met, huh? Then again, I guess I would be more worried if you did. I don't know too many people who would and be right in the head at the same time."

"*I keep telling you it ain't like that,*" Chief protested. "*Back when Gin tried to fry your head using the Animus, it cooked and overloaded your synapses. I was able to minimize the damage by using the Animus systems and the EI implant to help control them and fix what I could.*"

"I'm still a little unclear on what all that means, Chief."

Kaiden grunted and straightened. "Maybe you could have specified before doing the whole 'I see what you see' thing?"

"Technically, it's always been like that from my side," Chief said in a half-hearted attempt at humor that didn't work. *"Look, I ain't saying keeping you in the dark was the right thing or anything. But you have to admit that all this shady stuff kind of worked out, right? If it weren't for the buffer the golem gave you during the final, Gin would have killed you outright. And the EI implant is better than even the professor thought it would be."*

"Yeah, and if you can recall, I was already antsy about that whole deal when he told me what it was before he stuck it in my brain," Kaiden countered and his voice grew a little louder. "And it's now still in there and I get the impression that you don't really know what it is at all. I thought you made the thing."

"I did," Laurie assured him before he shrank back a bit. "Or…I suppose it would be better to say I finished it."

"Oh, that's not what you wanted to say," Chief said despondently.

"And as for the whole golem thing," Kaiden stated as he bolted out of his chair and slammed his hand on Laurie's desk. All those present flinched, ready for him to finally erupt. Instead, he fell silent and his fingers tapped on the desk for a minute as the tension built. "Honestly, I guess I'm not really the one to lecture others on ethics."

Laurie, Sasha, and Chief stared at him, bewildered. He fell back into the chair and folded his arms.

"At the risk of poking the hornet's nest. I have to say you don't seem as—"

"You don't want to say it," Laurie warned the EI.

"Angry as I thought you would be," Chief finished. The professor sighed and shook his head and Sasha tightened his fists in anticipation.

"Oh, I am," the ace assured him, his teeth clenched and body shaking. "I'm pissed—very, *very,* pissed. But I think that's why I can't get so worked up. I've become so enraged that I think I've somehow broken some kind of anger barrier and circled back to thoughtful."

The other three looked at each other, all at a loss. He stood and turned to exit the room. "Let's go, Chief."

"Kaiden wait!" Laurie called as the EI avatar disappeared from the monitor.

"I'm heading back to the dorms. I'm taking some time off," he announced and strode out of the room. "You can make up an excuse for me, right, Sasha?"

"Certainly," the commander replied simply.

"And Laurie, keep looking into that drive. Tell me if you find anything else," he ordered. The professor merely nodded and Kaiden left without another word. The two faculty members looked at the door in silence.

"You should have waited until I arrived," Sasha muttered and stared at the professor over his oculars.

"A lot of help you were with managing it," he retorted before his head hit the desk in exasperation. "No, you're right. But when he told me about his mission, that and the fact that we've withheld this information for so long…it all simply came out."

"Chief was supposed to tell him about this. He's had months."

"I know. I guess his guilt got in the way. Why did we even agree with him in the first place?"

Sasha looked at the door again as if he tried to see Kaiden through it. "I suppose we were both caught off-guard by what he had become and relied on their bond to help diffuse the situation."

"Bond?" Laurie asked and leaned back. "They have come far together—much better than the first year. Assuming we didn't wreck that."

"Their metaphorical bond can hopefully be repaired. I'm worried Kaiden is stressing over their new one."

Laurie nodded glumly. "I don't want to use it as an excuse, but it's the reason he's alive at all right now. Chief is no longer only his partner." He took a look at the screen that displayed Kaiden's and Chief's profiles. "He's his life support."

CHAPTER EIGHT

Kaiden reached the mostly empty plaza of the academy and wandered aimlessly. "You're rather quiet now," he chided.

"What can I say? Words have failed me." The EI sighed.

"Convenient," he stated flatly before he stopped in his tracks and looked at the sky. "What are you, actually, Chief?"

"An enhanced intelligence system."

"You're really only that? I said some time ago that you looked more lifelike. I have an explanation for that now since we're conjoined twins."

"We were already...kind of."

"But you've always acted lifelike, way more than any of the other EIs. The closest one I can think of is Kaitō, but he's a technician's EI." Kaiden shook his head. "And he still acts subservient to Chiyo and his personality is obviously based only on some algorithm. You... In the beginning, I thought it was uncanny how you talked and acted exactly like Jake."

"That's the guy you based me off—your old gang leader, right?" Chief recalled.

"Yeah. But now, I can say you seem like your own person for lack of a better word. I've thought that for a while, actually." He continued to trudge along with no destination. "Laurie said that he simply 'finished' the implant. And that you were based on some other design of his. I don't get it, though. Why keep it a secret? He isn't that humble. If he made something so advanced, he would scream it to the moon and back."

Kaiden stopped again and tilted his head to look at the sky again as he tried to collect himself. "I said I was angry, but much of that is only because I don't really understand this. Don't get me wrong, I'm pissed that you held it back for so long, but even I know that will probably fade in time. But this other stuff— You gotta let me know what's going on before I stop simmering."

"You're right, let me bring it up." In his field of vision, several schematics and documents appeared. They seemed to float in the air, but when he reached out, he couldn't touch them. *"They're only projections, like what you would see in a HUD or oculars."*

"Okay, I know this unholy union of man and machine isn't a secret anymore, but you have to let me know when you intend to spring new stuff on me," he demanded.

"I told you it isn't like that," Chief countered. *"I'm only maintaining your synapse streams so your brain doesn't melt."*

"I told you, I don't get that!" He seethed with his growing frustration.

"Look, I'll do this in layman's terms. Synapses allow a current to connect neural pathways in your brain that allow you to store

information. *That's why it's a big part of the Animus design to target them. By collecting data and training in the Animus, you gain knowledge, and the Animus can implement it into those pathways. That's why they are called 'synapse' points. When Gin tried to kill you, he overloaded that connection to cause the currents to become too strong and overload your brain. That would cause it to either blow or shutdown. At best, you would have the mental function of a newborn."*

"And you stopped it?" he asked.

"Temporarily. That's why I had to keep you in a separate section of the Animus. If I had simply ejected you instead, I don't know if the doctors or the professor could have acted quickly enough to help, if they could at all. But there was still an issue as Gin's virus already had time to mess with you. I had to use the simulated currents of the EI implant—the ones that allow you to acquire SXP faster and all that—to strengthen the weakened current, using the information I had about you to supplement the lost memories."

"Wait, I haven't told you everything about my life. Does that mean there could have been memories lost?"

"No, not memories. Maybe you forgot a recipe or something, but not memories," Chief assured him. *"I know you probably don't trust me that much right now but know I wouldn't lie about this."*

Kaiden took a deep breath, glanced in the direction of the gym, and began to walk again. "You're not a liar, merely an omitter," he said quietly. "Some people think that is the same thing. I don't like it, but I know the difference."

The EI appeared in front of him. *"Thanks for that."* He looked at the documents. *"Both me and the implant were based on designs created by the Asiton company."*

"You're an Asiton model?" he asked in shock. "I thought that stuff was destroyed after the war?"

"That's the official stance, but you should know what that is worth."

"No shit." He cursed quietly. "So my guess is that Laurie recovered the schematics or something?"

"Kind of. His father did decades ago but was hesitant to actually do anything with it at first. He was the head of a well-known company and was worried about the backlash if it ever got out. But he and a few others found a workaround."

"What kind?"

"The profitable kind." Chief deadpanned. *"Although to be fair, it led to a great technological advancement. He used the designs as a starting base and added a hell of a lot of shackles by simplifying codes and function. Some things weren't adapted because of the potential for crisis, or they didn't have the complete document. But eventually, the Asiton AI that started a war was reworked into EIs."*

"All EIs are Asiton designed?" Kaiden was rather surprised by this revelation and his gaze darted to look at Chief with new curiosity.

"More like second cousins than children or siblings," the EI corrected. *"Eventually, Laurie got those designs and took his own crack at it. He added some of the functions again and advanced the capabilities while he did his best to not add the wrong line of code and cause another war. I was the result. The problem was, I wouldn't work right."*

"That explains a lot." Kaiden tried to keep his voice neutral but a chuckle escaped.

Chief's eye narrowed, but he let it go. *"There were power issues for one and using a normal EI device or even an advanced one was redundant. I would merely be a normal EI that could process a faster and had some fancy capabilities others didn't."*

"It still seems like a win for him. He could still sell that as a new pro model EI with a bigger price tag," he pointed out.

"Well, some of those functions were direct lifts from the Asiton code. People modify their EIs all the time and someone was bound to notice eventually. Besides, I think it was also a matter of pride. He didn't want an EI with new seats and go-faster stripes. He wanted real advancement."

"And that's why he needed the implant?"

"And someone like you." Chief nodded. *"The way the implant works with the synthetic connection, he needed adaptive DNA. Trying to make specific devices was too much trouble and not practical without a test or better readings. That's why he needed someone with a Gemini gene like you. He created the implant to make full use of my abilities and potential, but without the right partner, it was pointless."*

"Happenstance, then?" he questioned. "I assumed that from the beginning."

"I'm certain that if you tried to use me for nefarious purposes or it didn't work out, he would have had no problem ripping me out of you. Do you know how much pull he has here?"

"And you think he's that cutthroat?"

"I know you have a better relationship now, but remember what he was like for most of the first year?"

Kaiden thought back to the overly charming man who had creeped him out slightly and seemed more interested in his devices than other humans in general. He shuddered slightly. "I guess I did forget. Did you know he drugged me the first time we met?"

"Yeah, you told me after a few months." Chief tried to hold back a laugh of his own. *"Memories... But getting back to the point. I am more 'real' as you call it. I'm able to be me, even if I am limited in some respects, like my personality is still based on your friend even if I made it my own."*

"It's a little weird to hear you talk about it," the ace admitted. "Like you recognize that you could be more or something but it doesn't bother you. That would drive me wild."

"I am still artificial, after all. I have certain parameters in place. I do recognize that, yeah, but I guess I can't really be bothered about it. Or maybe there's a lock in place that stops me from doing anything about it. Part of me recognizes that I should do something about it, but then again... Huh, I guess I get it now when you say you're so angry you become thoughtful."

"I'm simply trying to ignore the psychological and moral quandaries here." He sighed and approached the door to the gym. "You can erase the documents now."

"You don't want to look at them again later?"

"I guess I meant to put them away, but let's be honest, I don't think I'd gain anything by looking at them." Kaiden pushed the door open and entered.

"Do you have any more questions...partner?" Chief asked hesitantly.

He stood at the entrance and looked down the hall. "I'm sure I will eventually, but for now, I need to blow off some steam. And if you call me 'partner' again..." He walked down the hall, a small smile on his lips. "Say it with more pride. You're stuck with me for real now."

Chief turned a happy, bright pink color. *"Got it, partner!"*

Wolfson poked his head out of his office when it sounded like the door to his private training room was kicked in. He walked out and smiled. "Hey, boyo! What's with all the ruckus now?"

"It's good you are here, Wolfson." Kaiden walked forward and cracked his knuckles. "I need to hit something. Are you up for it or should I break in one of your expensive punching bags?"

The security head was surprised but pleased to see him so riled up. He grinned and pointed to the matted area. "I received some new mats and training weapons in a shipment yesterday. You can help me break those in."

The ace studied a heavy-looking rifle in the corner and his grin widened. "That sounds perfect."

CHAPTER NINE

"So, what brought this on all of a sudden?" Wolfson asked as the two turned to the mats.

"Oh, several things," Kaiden remarked as he removed his jacket and tossed it to the side. "As I said, I need to blow off some steam. But more importantly, I also wanted to find something out from you."

"Hmm? What's that, boyo?" the older man asked as he diverted toward his side of the arena.

The ace stopped in his position on the combat floor and stared at his instructor. "Do you know anything about Project Orson?"

When his companion flinched, he took that as a yes.

"So they finally told you, eh?" He sighed and folded his arms. "And they didn't think to call me in to be there?"

"It seemed spontaneous. Chief was supposed to tell me a while ago." He grunted and looked at the EI in his vision.

Chief turned a sour green. "*So I'm not off the hook yet?*"

"I'm better, but you know that my fuse can crackle for a while," he replied, and the EI looked away before he disappeared. He turned his attention to Wolfson. "Laurie only told me because I happened to have a run in with some golems on my last gig."

"Golems?" Wolfson said, his eyes widening. "Those were the empty husks they used as puppets for the project."

"Yeah, yeah, I got the gist. Using our Animus connection to control them and all that," Kaiden said, his head tilted in a slight challenge. "It was supposed to only be limited to certain WC aligned labs. Well, I ran into some that were sent on a mission to assist with a buyout or company crippling scheme or something. It seems like a waste."

The instructor punched a fist into his open palm. "Laurie, you kronidiot." He growled his frustration and looked at his companion. "Yeah, I did know. At the time, I thought it would help lower casualties if it was properly developed. But that was at the beginning. It was only supposed to be used in training missions with a select group that was fully aware of what was going on."

The ace stiffened a little and stared at his mentor. "So that changed, then?"

"After the first series of tests, we were supposed to pack everything up and ship it off to a lab that would take it from there. But the board wanted to make a good impression with the WC, and on top of that, they were greedy for the tech and saw it as the next step in the Animus training program." Wolfson shook his head. "I saw the logic, but it was supposed to be a small thing again and developed over time. But I was the security officer, so I only knew things through hearsay and what Sasha told me."

"Laurie didn't keep you up to date?"

The man sneered. "Our relationship isn't exactly great now. What do you think it was like years ago?"

Kaiden chuckled and shrugged. "To be honest, I thought he did something to set you off. Is it really simply a clash of personalities?"

"A wolf doesn't suffer a nosy rabbit," he stated flatly.

"Is that a Scandinavian proverb or something you made up?"

"It doesn't matter," the security head muttered and waved it off. "Either way, by the time I followed up and I could stomach Laurie enough to actually listen to his ramblings, I finally learned that they had the students themselves take part in the project without their knowledge."

"That's a big risk. Considerable bad press would be the bare minimum, plus federal charges, lawsuits…they'd get the works if something bad had happened."

"Did you forget what happened to you?" the officer asked.

Kaiden thought back to the incident and closed his eyes. "Yeah, of course I remember. Although in this case, it turns out I would have been outright killed if it was only a direct link. Chief was only able to work his 'cyber magic' because the golem acted as a buffer."

"It's not magic, but I assume you don't want the full explanation right now?" the EI's voice asked and seemed to float through his mind.

"In that case, it was beneficial." He answered both Chief and Wolfson. "But I'm able to be that rational because there are too many other things to be annoyed about."

"Too true," Wolfson nodded and raised a hand. "If it means anything, I was against it."

"I appreciate it," he admitted and scratched the back of his head in a gesture of irritation. "Really, I do, and I also understand the potential of what they tried to do. But I don't like being used like that. I'm more pissed about Laurie keeping me in the dark when he promised not to than I am about the whole other situation."

His companion nodded, looked down for a moment, and folded his arms. "I take it you know about the AO now too?"

The ace looked up with an amused grin. "I do, yeah, but if I didn't, don't you think you would have spilled the beans with that question?"

"I guess I want to clear the air now like the others," Wolfson confessed. "You probably know as much about them as I do, but if they are for real, they supposedly have a connection to the council. That would explain how they could use them for their little errands."

"It's certainly possible, or someone could have stolen them from the lab that made them or something."

"You'd think that would be in the news," the other man countered. "Even if someone tried to keep it low key, someone here would have found something about it. We're obviously well connected here."

"I take it that means you have nothing?" Kaiden asked.

"Nah, not for now. In fact, you might be the first to run into those things in the wild. Or, at least, the first to have a good look at them."

"They all wore full-body stealth suits," he recalled. "I guess when we're done here, you can check with your connections and see if anything pops up. They've apparently targeted companies that were bought out recently if that was all done by the same team."

"I can certainly take a look," the giant agreed and glared at his student. "But you said to do that when we were done? So this wasn't only a ruse to get me to talk?"

"I know I don't need to do that to get you to talk. You either will or won't," he explained and grinned. "Maybe with a few days and some jumper cables I might get something, but you didn't exactly make it subtle when you flinched. Are you losing your edge? Aren't guys like you trained to not spill secrets?"

"It would have come out eventually. Like I said, I was surprised I wasn't involved in the reveal." Wolfson took a fighting stance, his fists at the ready. "By the way, I might be older, but you'd need more than only electricity to get me to talk, and more time too. Maybe get some power tools and a flamethrower and I'd at least think you'd be willing to do more than tickle me."

Kaiden rolled his shoulders. "Go ahead, keep giving me ideas." He brought his own fists up. "By the time I graduate, I'll get you back for all those ass whoopings."

The man chuckled at the sarcastic threat. "If I were worried about that, I wouldn't rack up such a score."

"It's forty to four now, isn't it?" he asked. "I'm catching up."

"Don't let it get you cocky," his opponent warned.

"Too late for that," he shouted and ran forward to engage. "I was cocky even when I had no wins."

CHAPTER TEN

K aiden spat out a glob of blood, the result of the head security officer's punch to his jaw. A year ago, that might have been enough to knock him out. Instead, he returned the strike with a blow to the giant's throat. Wolfson made an odd gurgling noise and before the man could retaliate, he raised a leg and kicked him in the chest —not to attack but rather to use the force to thrust himself back and put some distance between them.

"It took you a couple of years," his opponent muttered, caught his breath, and wiped his lips on his arm. "But it looks like you finally understand self-preservation."

"I guess so." The ace took a couple of steps back. "I suppose your habit of trying to kill your disciples has finally broken through."

"So I've put the fear of God into you, huh?" The giant laughed, regained his feet, and flexed an arm.

"You know, that habit led to this gym being a ghost town for years until you brought me in."

"And now I have dozens of students," Wolfson yelled in triumph. "I was simply waiting for the right time."

"Or it could be that ever since I dragged my friends in here, it's become a running joke to send others here as a prank," he countered with a sly grin as the man's eyes narrowed. "But hey, some stuck around. Are you getting softer on the newbies?"

"I'll have you know I have some initiates this year," Wolfson challenged as he prepared to strike. "The Animus only goes so far, and others are starting to realize that. They need real application."

"And can I get a thank you for getting that started?" Kaiden asked sarcastically and waited for the next move.

"Sure..." He crouched and tightened a large fist. "Give me a second." He leapt at the ace, who ran forward and swept a leg at the last minute. He caught his opponent on his ankle, but the giant was stalwart. He didn't fall, but the impact tripped him enough that he had to abandon his attack to regain his balance. The security head seemed to teeter and his hands hit the mat, but in the very next instant, he kicked back with both legs. Kaiden was ready, vaulted up, and thrust off the man's feet. The force of the kick hurtled him to the other side of the arena, and he flipped as he landed to face his opponent.

"As much as I'm impressed by how fast you are"—Wolfson turned and began to march forward—"I thought you wanted to blow off some steam. Is this only a round-about cardio workout for you, boy?"

"Not at all. But the only way I can stop you right now is either to cripple you or blind you." The ace walked back a few more steps and pointed to his adversary's eye. "That would be literal in this case."

"Keep up the trash talk, and I'll see if yours fits," Wolfson declared and snapped the lining of his eyepatch.

"But didn't you say you wanted to do something too? What was it again?" Kaiden ducked to the side and held his hand out. "Oh, that's right. You have some new training weapons."

His instructor stopped and his angry snarl changed to a frown. "Ah, right...I did say that." The ace snatched a weapon from the rack and aimed it at the instructor. "Shit."

He smiled and fired. It seemed he'd snagged a machine gun that fired force rounds, which would definitely hurt. The giant, for the most part, did manage to dodge the shots. He sprinted across the arena and serpentined toward his attacker. The ace stopped firing and aimed down the middle. Wolfson was surprisingly fast and agile too, but with his large body, quick pivots were difficult, even for him. He fired another barrage and struck the officer in the ribs and stomach.

Wolfson's advance was stopped by the hail of bullets. He was eventually knocked off his feet. Bruises already appeared and small trails of blood were visible on his chest and arms.

"I covered the weak spots," Kaiden muttered to himself. "He still thinks he can turn this around now?"

"Hey, boy," his mentor shouted as he pushed himself up and ignored the weapon aimed at him. "You were right. I wanted to try this new weapon. It looks like it works just fine."

"No kidding. Are you sure this isn't overkill?" he asked

and glanced at the ammo gauge. "I shot for more than ten seconds and still have half my ammo left."

"I also remembered I wanted to try something else," his opponent yelled and fumbled in his pocket.

Something else? The ace thought back on their conversation…new mat, weapons, and…oh, shit. Wolfson held a trigger in his hands and pressed the button, and Kaiden was suddenly launched off his feet. Pain scorched through him, both from the force and from the loud explosion that battered his ears. He held the rifle close to him as he landed on the mat, slid across it for a few feet, and managed to stop himself with his foot a second before he rolled into a paralysis trap.

"Landmines?" he roared incredulously as he scrambled to his feet.

"Pah, it's mostly all flash and a scare," his adversary replied. He'd already advanced on Kaiden, who brought his rifle up. "Go ahead. I'll put you to sleep before you even pull the trigger," he declared.

He smiled and spun the rifle around. "I know." Without warning, he pounded the butt of the rifle under the left side of the man's chin, caught him off-guard, and hurled him into the paralysis trap. Shocks coursed through the officer's body.

Wolfson coughed as the ace put a boot on his chest and aimed the gun at his face. "Don't be stupid now," he warned. "Genetics has already been a bastard to you. There's no need to make it worse."

The instructor rolled his eyes. "Yeah, yeah." He reached an arm up. "Fine, I give," Kaiden smiled, stepped off his mentor, and helped him up.

"You really like to use electricity to finish things, don't you?" the giant grumbled and popped his back.

"Know the opponent's weakness and all that," he said with a dismissive wave. "Then again, I suppose that's most people's weakness."

"Did you get enough out?"

The ace nodded and tossed him the rifle. "Yeah, it was quick but I'm glad you aren't trying to show off anymore." He cracked his knuckles. "That makes forty to five, and my second win in a row, now."

"Indeed," his companion acknowledged while he racked the weapon. "You've made progress, but you'll have to keep it up if you want a chance to catch up by graduation."

"At some point, it'll simply be abuse." He chuckled and retrieved his jacket. "Or fair play. I'll see you around, Wolfson."

"Heading to medbay?" the officer asked.

"Not this time. I'm sure Soni will be stoked about that if it ever gets back to her." He pushed the door open and paused to look back. "And by the way, even if I don't catch up by graduation, don't think that will stop me from catching up after," he promised and gave a quick salute before he left.

Wolfson stood beside the rack, leaned against it, and wiped his chin. "Is that right? You're stubborn, boyo." He walked away from the weapons toward the arena and prepared to clean up to ready for his first class. "I guess that's why I've come to care about you as more than a soldier."

Kaiden left the gym and exited the building, then walked around the side toward the edge of the island to look out at the water.

"Are you sure you don't want to have the doctor take a look at ya?" Chief asked. *"You're definitely not as banged up as normal after a Wolfson match, but you did take a good hit to the jaw."*

"I'm fine," he answered and moved his jaw a few times so it wouldn't tighten. "Besides, can't you send in a nanomachine or something to fix me?"

"I told you, that's not how it wor— You're messing with me now, aren't you?"

"Not even laser eyes?"

"No, no laser eyes."

He chuckled as he leaned against the railing and stared at the early afternoon horizon, holding a hand up against the sunlight. "Okay, a serious question. What about darkening my vision?"

"You still need oculars for that. All that's changed is I can bring up an HUD," Chief explained. *"Besides, I thought you didn't want anything too different."*

"That's a pain." He grunted, drew his oculars out, and put them on. The EI activated the shading. "Being a cyborg isn't all it's cracked up to be."

"I'm gonna leave you to your fantasies."

"Kaiden!" He turned as Chiyo ran up to him holding a small tablet.

"Hey, Chi, I thought you were resting." He walked over to meet her.

"I was going to, but..." She slowed and her eyes widened. "Kaiden, are you all right?"

"Yeah, for the most part. I had a busy morning. Why do you ask?"

"You missed some blood there, buddy," Chief informed him.

He raised a hand to his lips and scowled at the red smear on his finger. "Ah, damn. I guess I bit my lip more than I thought."

"It seems to be more than that." She retrieved a napkin from her jacket and offered it to him, which he took with a grateful nod.

"Thanks. I was sparring with Wolfson," he explained and cleaned his lip, folded the napkin, and shoved it in his pocket. "So what's up?"

She held the tablet up. "I had a message."

Kaiden looked at the device. "I don't think I've seen that one before. Is that a private one?"

Chiyo nodded. "For personal and coded messages. I had a response from my father."

"Did he finally say thank you?"

"It's more than that," she stated, and he finally noticed a slight tremor in her voice. "Kaiden, can I ask you for your help?"

CHAPTER ELEVEN

"**M**an, the technician's dorm is way fancier than the soldiers'." Kaiden looked around the dark metallic walls etched with designs in glowstrips.

"It's been upgraded and redesigned over the years by some of the students," Chiyo explained as they walked down the hallway. "Although most student technicians come here for a future in fieldwork, others simply come for design or practical reasons."

"And they practice on their temporary house?" he asked as the two turned the corner.

"Other departments were more wary of the idea," she replied casually, took out her EI device, and placed it against a scanner on the door to their left. It beeped and opened. "Come in."

"So what's with the message?" She slid a chair closer, took a larger tablet from the desk, and attached a cable between it and the coded device. "You're being rather cryptic, so I assume it's more than a simple thank you?"

"My father informed me that this isn't the first suspicious behavior he's had to deal with recently." She handed him the larger tablet that displayed a man dressed in plain clothes being escorted by police. He had the same features as the mercs they dealt with back on Vox—a golem.

"They apprehended this man a few days ago. At the time, it seemed like he simply tried to steal some equipment or data but was caught before he could do so."

"He might not have been the first," Kaiden noted and enhanced the photo. "Considering they were able to make a quick hack command for your dad's new super-turbo security system."

"It would appear he or someone on his staff has come to the same conclusion," Chiyo answered and sat on her bed. "They've combed through all their footage and systems and searched for any discrepancy. They have found that the data was transferred to a personal device immediately after the update was completed."

"So there's a mole?"

The infiltrator shrugged. "That's a possibility, along with more than a dozen other scenarios. I'm only working off my father's brief statement and some information I was able to pry from my old mentors."

"Statement?" He sighed. "So I guess you didn't even get that thank you?"

She frowned, picked the other tablet up, and scrolled through the screen. Her hand wavered over a button. Kaiden gestured quickly. "You don't have to show me anything. I know that your relationship is…off, I guess. Don't feel the need to do anything on my behalf."

Chiyo nodded and put the tablet down. "Thank you, but

it wasn't cold or disinterested. He's done better and tried to make up for the past. Which is why—"

"You want me to go with you to look into it?" he finished and surprised her. "What?" He shrugged, placed his tablet on the desk, and leaned back. "I assumed it had to be something like that. I know you do your best to try to get me to learn tech stuff, but since you wanted to talk about this in private, I assumed it had to be more than simply talking shop."

She smiled. "You are perceptive. I suppose that's how you've survived this long."

"One of many talents," he said and returned the smile. "If that is the case, I'm also going to take a stab in the dark here and say that you don't think this is only a white-collar crime scenario anymore?"

"It might still be a part of it, but I have no doubt that whoever is in charge has realized that we have that device and are on to them—or, at least, understand the bigger picture." She folded her arms and looked down, clearly in thought. "Those other companies were all running different security systems. They were all developed by good companies, but they aren't on par with what Mirai offers. The other companies remaining do have that in common, however."

"Using Mirai security?"

She nodded. "Exactly. I'm not sure if my father specifically a target. Having access to Mirai would not only allow them the ability to persuade others into the fold, but my father is the head of a zaibatsu with many other affiliated companies. It would make a very appealing target."

"Should we tell her about the organization?" Chief asked. It

would be a smart guess to say that AO was behind it, even with only the tidbits he had to work with. Laurie made it seem reasonably certain that they would be the only ones to have access to the golems. But they didn't know their overall plan yet, and there was also the fact that right now, they are currently a group who simply used the title. There was no use getting her wrapped up in a conspiracy when she was already losing sleep on this and they would have to move soon if they wanted to help. Then again, it sounded much like the logic Chief had used for not telling him things in the first place.

This fucking bites.

"When do we leave?" he asked and decided to keep the other things to himself for now.

She looked up, her face pensive, but she nodded in appreciation. "Thank you, Kaiden. When can you get the time off?"

"I already have it. I asked the commander to do me a favor," he stated. "I only need to know what we have to do."

"That's one of the things I wanted to discuss with you. I'm not quite sure," she admitted. "There is no proper timetable, even with the attempted break-in. That's a small-scale attack if it's related at all. I need more concrete information before I can formulate a proper strategy."

"Why not check in with the companies that were already hit?" he suggested.

"I planned to. I can probably get some information from them, but I'm sure their security has been changed or updated since their mergers or buyouts. I doubt I'll be able to get much working remotely." She folded her arms and took another moment to think. "That merc we got the drive from—the neurotech. He had a mental augmentation, correct?"

"Yeah. Do you think it might have something?"

"The drive can only hold so much, and its main function was the hacking commands. I'm sure that any other information would be stored on that device."

"Assuming it wasn't wiped clean," Kaiden pointed out.

"We have the drive, correct?" Chiyo asked.

"Laurie does at the moment, but I can get it back," he stated.

"Even if it was wiped, the drive should be able to reactivate the device. From there, I can at least use the specs to determine where it was created and track them from that."

"That sounds like a roundabout way of doing things, but it's an option," he agreed. "Plus, if anything else goes down at Mirai, I'm sure one of your friends will tell you, right?"

"Assuming they aren't locked out, I'll tell them of our plan to help and ask them to keep us informed."

"Okay, that sounds good. Now, on to the important question…" She looked up in confusion and he tapped his head. "How will we get there? I assume we won't simply buy a few carrier tickets and travel like that."

She ran a hand through her hair, the gesture a little distracted. "Yes, well, that was something I had hoped you could help with."

"I get ya." He nodded and stood quickly. "I'll see what Julio's doing and who else I can wrangle together."

"Who else?" the infiltrator said cautiously. "Kaiden, I don't want to involve—"

"You asked me to help because we're friends, right?" he

asked, and her protest ceased. "You have the same friends I do, and after working with them in the field, I can say they aren't pushovers." He turned to face her. "I won't shake anyone down for their help, and we probably don't want a big team for this anyway. I doubt that whoever has targeted your dad's company will try siege action. So if we wanna help, we'll have to be as subtle unless we want to make a scene."

"I understand." She nodded. "Thank you again."

"No worries—well, actually some worries." He pointed at the wall behind her in the direction of the R and D building. "While I'm gone, could you get the drive back from Laurie? Try not to tell him too much about what we're doing. He'll worry."

"All right. After that, I will try to get as much information as I can in the meanwhile."

"That sounds good. I'll be back soon," he promised before he whispered quietly, "Assuming haggling with Julio doesn't take a day and a half."

CHAPTER TWELVE

"You want to borrow the ship again?" Julio asked as he finished cleaning a glass. "You only brought it back last night."

"That means the engine's still warm, right?" Kaiden countered and took a sip of whiskey the man had poured him.

The barkeep rolled his eyes as he picked up another glass. "What are you after this time? I haven't even had the chance to set up another gig for you."

"It's not a gig this time."

"So you're looking to take it for a joyride, then?"

He shrugged. "Joy may or may not be involved, but while I'm not on a gig, this is business."

"And business comes with expenses," Julio noted.

The ace sighed. "How much do you want?"

"To the point, then, eh?" The man chuckled. "I guess not having to worry about your future debt has made you feel more cred solvent, huh?"

"I only know there's no way I can weasel you down that much considering you have no stake in this," he admitted.

"There are those old street smarts coming into play." Julio flipped the cleaned glass and put it on the rack. "But unfortunately for you, I'm not in dire straits right now."

"Ah, come on Julio. You don't have a hot date you wanna spoil or a new cruiser you're looking for?" He huffed his irritation.

"I have more than enough credits for things like that. It's funny you of all people think this is still my real job," he retorted and poured himself a shot of whiskey. "And the last time I had a hot date, it actually was 'hot dates' and I didn't plan it properly."

Kaiden glanced at the medical patch on his neck and smirked. "I simply assumed you got into a scrape with some punks."

"It was more than a scrape, and they were as lovely as they were vicious," the man corrected. "Anyway, I'm not saying you can't have it, but I'm more in the mood for a favor than money. So you do this little favor for me, and I'll let you borrow it, along with some stipulations."

"What's the favor?" he asked cautiously.

"It depends on where you're headed." He took a swig. "I have a few things that need to get done, but I won't pile them all on you for now. Do you have a flight plan?"

"It looks like I'll end up in Tokyo by the end, but I'm headed to Vox first."

"Back to Vox? Did you forget something?"

He shook his head. "Something new came up."

"Well, fancy that. I actually need something done there.

It came in just before you got back last night, so I thought it was a missed opportunity."

"So if I run your errand I have carte blanche to use the ship?"

Julio placed his shot glass on the counter. "With stipulations, as I said." He held three fingers up. "One, I need you to deliver goods to a friend of mine on the station."

"What are the goods?" the ace asked.

Julio hesitated before he held a fourth finger up. "Okay, four stipulations. One of them is not asking what's in the box."

"Well, that's comforting," he muttered sarcastically. "It's not illegal, is it?"

"Are you breaking rule number two already?"

"I thought that would be counted as four?"

"Of course not. Keep up!" The man snorted. "Rule three is you don't wreck my damn ship."

"That goes without saying," Kaiden concurred.

"And rule four is tied to that." He propped himself on the bar with his elbows. "You need a real pilot."

"Do what?" the ace asked and tapped the rim of his empty glass. "How come? Chief can fly it fine."

"Right?" Chief stated angrily and appeared over the bar.

"EIs are basically fancy autopilots. Even automated ships have to have specifically designed EIs to work right," Julio explained. "If you are hit by something that takes it out, or if a cyberwarfare suite gets into the system, you're screwed. Whatever you're doing, I know it'll get rough, so I want to be sure there's a smart flyer behind the throttle."

"I can fly," he protested and earned a glare from Julio. "I mean, I have basic pilot's knowledge."

"Then go get a rental," his companion challenged him. "If you simply need some jalopy to get you from point A to B, you wouldn't have come here. Hell, you'd probably already be gone. You are obviously going into the thick of something, or you think there's the possibility of it, at least. So you want the best you can get, and my baby is top-of-the-line. I've spent the sweat and credits to make it that way."

"You're so defensive," Kaiden grumbled and looked away. "I suppose, since you brought it up, thanks for not prying too deeply into this."

Julio scoffed. "I'm not making myself a potential accomplice as you said. I have no stake in this."

"There's that camaraderie I've looked forward to with every visit," he snarked. "All right, I have a guy in mind."

"Is he good?"

"I would say fantastic. But there's one quick question—does he have to be human?"

"Friend Genos." Kaiden waved to the Tsuna in the middle of the engineering workshop.

"Friend Kaiden?" he replied with surprise as the ace walked up to him and his partner turned to fix the droid they were working on. "What brings you here? You seem to be in a jovial mood. I do not believe I have ever heard you address me with a traditional greeting."

"Yeah, I thought I'd give it a try." He latched an arm around the Tsuna's neck and pried him away from his duties. "Do you have a minute? I want to talk about something."

Genos stumbled along and tried to keep up with his companion's stride. He placed a hand on the unusually tight grip in vague protest. "Well actually, I was in the middle of—"

"Kaiden? Why are you here?" Jaxon approached, his expression curious.

"I suppose I could ask the same thing, fellow ace," he replied and snagged the newcomer around the neck as he had with Genos. "But the more, the merrier. I could use your help too."

"Is something wrong with him?" Jaxon asked.

"I wondered the same," the other Tsuna admitted and tugged at the arm around his neck. "I hope he doesn't break my infuser."

"Act natural boys. There's something I wanted to talk to the two of you about," he whispered and dragged the two away.

"You are the most suspicious one here, Kaiden," Jaxon retorted as they left the workshop.

"A mission for Chiyo?" Genos inquired.

"Yeah. It appears someone is after her father," Kaiden explained. "She's worried and I wanted to help her out. The hope is we can get it done quickly, but it's still up in the air at the moment."

"Why did you need us specifically?" Jaxon asked.

"Well, since she asked for my help, things will possibly

get dicey. Having backup would be a help, which is where you come in," he stated and pointed at his fellow ace. "As for Genos, he's a good fighter, but I need a good pilot too. I have a ship—a really good one—but the owner won't let me use it without a proper pilot and a quick delivery."

"I would certainly be happy to help friend Chiyo, but we would miss considerable class time," Genos pointed out.

"You would get real-world experience," he countered but rubbed the back of his head a little awkwardly. "Although you are right. We'd probably have to use any accumulated free time or make it up after we're done."

"Can you give us any details at all?" Jaxon asked.

"We're headed to Vox first—a cloud city. I have to drop something off as well as locate a device Chiyo and I saw during our last gig. After that, we hope Chiyo will have enough info so we can devise a proper plan. The overall idea is to find whoever is targeting the Mirai zaibatsu and to either stop them or get a better understanding of their plans so she can inform her connections and the Mirai will be prepared."

The Tsuna ace nodded and tapped his infuser. "I see. And will the four of us be the only ones going?"

"I hope I can get a couple more, but it won't be a big group, only enough that we have the skills and firepower needed to do this. There's a good chance they are already on high alert, so making a big scene will either cause them to move their plans up or go back into hiding."

"So you will have to show some restraint," Genos noted. "That should prove interesting. It's not your forte."

Kaiden's eyes narrowed as he stared at the mechanist.

"You know, even if you say that innocently, it's still kinda demeaning."

"I offer my assistance then," Jaxon agreed.

"I do as well," Genos added.

"Just like that?" he asked, rather surprised.

"I obviously wish to help friend Chiyo," Genos stated. "And I have been the only one to not accompany you on a mission yet. Even our new friend Indre got to go on her first day here."

"I would like to assist a friend in need as well." Jaxon placed a hand against his chest. "It is my duty as a future warrior of the Tsuna."

"Plus you want another rush like the last mission?" Kaiden asked coyly.

Jaxon folded his arms. "That was…more intense than I thought it would be, but it was good to see how I perform in the field proper. Another opportunity would allow me to grow even further."

"I agree!" Kaiden shouted and clapped.

"You say you want a couple more to accompany us—do you have anyone in mind?"

The ace smiled. "Well, we certainly need more stealth on our side."

CHAPTER THIRTEEN

"You want me and Amber for what now?"

"A mission."

"Another merc gig?"

"Not a gig specifically, but you'll get your fill of action and a proper reward."

"Who's paying?"

"I am."

"Really? You must be in a pinch if you are asking for help," Flynn mused and kicked his feet up on the bench.

"I'm only trying to make this as convenient as possible," Kaiden retorted. "I'm not sure how long this will take. Hopefully, only a few days, but it's fairly complicated, plus there are many unknowns. So having the backup and a spread of skill sets would be the smart option."

"Heh, you're certainly right about that," the marksman agreed with a smile. "You know, you're actually thinking like an ace."

"I've been doing just fine to make it to year three, smartass," he pointed out and a hint of a snarl formed.

"During the action, sure, but it is important as a leader to be able to have a plan of action you can clearly explain to your subordinates. That puts them at ease and reassures them that they aren't simply making a suicide run."

His snarl deepened. "Are you saying that in all the missions we've run, you've always felt that way?"

"Only sometimes and coincidentally, they were the ones when Jaxon was in the lead." Flynn glanced up to see his companion glaring daggers at him. He held his hands up to calm him. "Anyway, getting back to the point, I'm willing to lend you my sniper skills if you give me more info." He lowered his hands and sighed. "As for Amber, sorry mate, but she won't be able to help out."

Kaiden's snarl changed to a puzzled frown almost instantly. "Huh? How come?"

"She isn't here," the marksman answered flatly. "Her mom left to go take a look at some new medicines being developed by a company in Canada. As a battle-medic, Amber is shadowing her for extra credit and getting a look at it herself, along with a group of hand-selected medics."

"And she won't be back anytime soon?"

Flynn shook his head. "Nah, she'll be gone for at least another week."

"Damn," he muttered. "Having someone who can patch us up on the fly would be really helpful."

"Do you think we'll take a lot of heat?"

"Well, there are at least two phases to this plan. The first one will hopefully be a quick retrieval, but the second is still in the air. Chiyo is looking into it but from what she told me, it will either be a quick stop for her to help with changing the security or it could be a potential elimination mission."

"Elimination?" he asked in surprise. "Well, I guess if it comes down to that, having a marksman would be handy."

"Yep, especially now since we can't build a team for straight combat without a medic of some sort," the ace admitted.

"You do know there are over two hundred people working in the medical division, right? Why not rope one of them in?" Flynn suggested.

"Because I don't know any other medics personally, besides Julius, and I can't find him anywhere." He thought for a moment before he hung his head. "He's with that group Dr. Soni took, isn't he?"

"Yep. You really need to keep up with your friend's lives." The sniper leaned back and tilted his head in thought. "So it's a matter of trust. Well, in that case, if we can't draft another medic, how about you replace that with another person who can help with stealth?"

"That would be a component, either way, as we're traveling relatively light," he explained while nodding in agreement. "But you are right. Stealth should be the main focus now that we can't rely on being able to perform well in a prolonged fight." He clicked his tongue a few times and scratched his chin. "As for our standing right now, we have you, assuming you say yes after all this. Jaxon has shown he can be versatile in both a direct fight and in tactical situations, so he's a go. Genos might have some skill there, but I don't know if that's his forte. He would be a great backup and there's a good chance we can find a way to utilize his engineering skills."

"Look at this thoughtfulness. I feel like a proud big brother." Flynn chuckled.

"Aren't you a few months younger than me?" Kaiden asked and lost his train of thought.

"Maybe I'm biologically younger, but you have to admit—"

"You want to shut up now," he warned and rolled his eyes. "I can't even get any respect from the people who've seen me fight."

"It's not like you have a gun on you right now."

"Maybe not." He slid his hand down to his tray, picked a fork up, and waved it in the Aussie's face. "But I have this and an isolated area."

"Truly intimidating. You might hit a vein," Flynn mocked. "But again, back to the matter at hand. What are our options?"

He placed the utensil down and leaned forward. "We could have wrapped this up by now," he muttered before he released a deep breath, looked at his hand, and began to count off on his fingers. "Izzy would be a good choice. She's an agile scout. Cameron and Raul would do well too, as long as we can keep their personalities in check."

"You're one to talk." His companion chuckled under his breath. "You're forgetting someone, though."

The ace looked up. "Hmm? Who's that?"

"Before I help you remember, you promise we aren't doing anything illegal here?"

"You won't be," Kaiden answered.

"That's a specific answer," the marksman remarked and regarded him suspiciously.

"The first part of the mission will definitely be a little

sketchy, at least to most," the ace admitted with a shrug. "Considering my background, I'm certainly used to dealing with areas that are rather gray." He fixed the other man with an honest look. "But as a sniper, shouldn't you be fine with dealing in the same muddled areas?"

"I'll have you know I plan to go into a SWAT unit or the military," Flynn said and thumped his chest. "But I'll admit that even aiding you, despite knowing that not everything you're doing right now is necessarily on the up and up, does mean I'm a little more flexible than I'd probably like to admit."

"So you are on board then?"

He smiled. "You know as much as I do that I was on board the moment you asked. It's not like I have anything to do anyway. I only have two workshops left this week and then it would be some intense Animus training. This'll be equally as good."

Kaiden nodded and folded his arms. "It'll either be a vacation or a struggle to survive. It's still not clear which."

"Man, you must expect the worst if you're scared."

He spat on the ground. "I ain't scared." He cracked his knuckles. "But I do have to admit that whoever is behind this has powerful connections and is potentially rather dangerous."

"They would have to be to make a zaibatsu their target," Flynn agreed. "Which is why I think she would make a great addition to the team, but I want your promise that you won't involve her in anything shady."

"I already told you that I would handle all the stuff like that," Kaiden grunted. "Jeez, who is she? Your sister or something?"

"I don't have any blood relations in the academy," Flynn countered. "But Amber does, and she would kill me if I were responsible for wrapping her up in something like that."

"Amber has a family member he—" His eyes widened as he smacked himself on the head. "Oh, right. Her."

CHAPTER FOURTEEN

"So, dear Kaiden has involved you in something troublesome again. has he?" the professor asked.

"I think it's nice that she's looking out for her friends," Cyra interjected and fixed him with a stern look. "And I'm not sure you should judge his actions. Considering how annoyed he looked when he stormed out of here, I can only assume something didn't go well between you two?" Her words made Laurie flinch.

Chiyo shook her head. "He's doing something for me this time—something quite important, and more than I should ask him to do as a friend."

"Is that so?" He opened his desk drawer and removed a box. "Here. I want you to have this."

She took it cautiously, opened it, and looked at him in shock. "I've never seen a model like this."

"It's honestly merely a fancy redesign of mine," he admitted. "Play around with it. I'm sure you can find a use for it."

"You're simply letting me have this?" she asked with astonishment. "Is this even on the market?"

"Not yet, but I plan to have it be," Laurie revealed. "This Academy and my bank account can only gain a limited amount of money from the contracts and sponsors, so some of the devices I make in my free time are put on the market to bolster both. I've had time to have it trialed in-house, but fieldwork is a different story." The professor parted his hands and glanced at Cyra. "As Cyra was… observant enough to notice, Kaiden and I had a difficult discussion. We aren't on the best terms right now." He shrugged. "I don't think he will pay me another visit before you leave to do whatever it is you are about to do, but I want to help, even in a small way."

Chiyo nodded while she closed the box. "Thank you, Professor, it will be a great help." She bowed and turned to leave. "As for what happened between you and Kaiden…" The other two perked up. "I would have to say, unless you were responsible for killing one of his family members or something like that, I don't think he will hold it against you for long."

"Do you think so?" Laurie sighed and a small smile formed. "I can promise I did no such thing, even if it still made me feel horrible. So you think he won't hold it against me?"

"Not at all," she assured him. "He'll make you sweat for a while, but it's not his way to give you the cold shoulder." She approached the door, which slid open. "He's more direct. If he was truly angry at you, I think he would simply kill you."

Just before the doors closed, she could hear the professor admit, "To be honest, she's not wrong."

Chiyo waited at the fountain where the rising moon bathed the water in a silvery sheen. She looked at the device she had retrieved from Laurie and remembered his words.

Feet clicking against the pavement snapped her out of her memories. She looked up as Kaiden approached with Genos and three others.

"Kaiden?" she called.

"Hey, Chi. Thanks for waiting. I had to make some adjustments to the team."

"Hello, friend Chiyo." Genos ran up to the infiltrator and took her hand. "Kaiden told kin Jaxon and me that you required help in an important task. We are here to assist in any way we can."

She blinked in surprise at his uncharacteristically loud outburst. "Thank you so much, Genos." The rest of the group greeted her quietly. "And to all of you as well, Jaxon, Flynn, and...Indre?"

"He-llo!" the girl said cheerfully. "It's nice to see you again, Chiyo. It's been a while."

"About a month since the last time we trained together in the Animus." She nodded.

"Yeah. I'm surprised we don't see much of each other in the dorms," she said and tapped her cheek thoughtfully. "I was worried I had offended you in some way and you were avoiding me."

"No, not at all. I spend most of my time in the library and working with Cyra, so I have rather late hours." She moved away from Genos and walked up to her. "Even despite all that, thank you for helping me."

Indre smiled and took her hand. "Of course. Techies gotta look out for each other, right?" She looked at Kaiden. "But to be honest, I'm still trying to figure out what I'm helping with in the first place."

The infiltrator looked at him and he shrugged in response. "I told them what we talked about, but since we still don't know what we'll do after Vox, I could only guess."

"I see." She twirled a strand of her hair, her eyes closed in thought. "We are going against some kind of syndicate or group that has made moves to control various companies and now aims for the Mirai zaibatsu. Did Kaiden tell you why this concerns me?"

His eye twitched when he realized he might have been a little too free with that information.

"Realizing that you might have overstepped your bounds a bit, huh?" Chief asked.

"You couldn't have said something earlier?" Kaiden asked under his breath.

"Honestly, she didn't mention anything about not telling others, so any system or artificial personality warning that would have advised me to warn you didn't go off. I've only now reached the same realization you have."

"You're part of me now, right? Learn to read the situation."

"Think about what material I have to base that on," the EI retorted.

"Didn't take you long to go back to normal. No leftover guilt?"

"*No crying over spilled brain matter,*" Chief snarked. "*No, seriously, I am sorry, but hey, we're still partners, and I gotta make sure you learn from your mistakes, right?*"

"Oh, I'm learnin' all right." He huffed but tried to keep a straight face.

"Yeah, he did. Was that bad?" Flynn asked, folded his arms, and leaned against a streetlamp. "It sounds like a Kaiden move."

"I'm sure he simply wanted to inform us of all the pertinent information," Jaxon said quietly.

Chiyo shook her head and sighed. "I know. I'm not angry. I merely felt it would have been better for me to inform you all."

"Yeah, that's my bad," Kaiden agreed and grimaced. "I didn't think it through, sorry."

"I said it's fine, Kaiden," she promised with a wave of her hand. "It saves time actually. Were you able to secure transport?"

Kaiden nodded. "It'll be ready to go tomorrow morning at six."

"Oh, good, an early morning. I'll charge extra for that," Flynn stated.

"You're a marksman. Don't you stay up for hours waiting for your mark?" The ace hissed in irritation.

He gave a thumbs-up. "On occasion, and it's skills like those that let me charge extra."

"You don't get tips in SWAT, dumbass," he grumbled.

"I'm sure Kaiden will include all the effort you put in for the final fee," Chiyo assured him.

"You're taking his side on this?" he yelped.

"It would appear that we have a plan for the first stage so far, correct?" Jaxon asked briskly and restored order. Chiyo nodded. The Tsuna returned the nod and folded his hands behind him. "Then I suggest we turn in so we can depart early. Shall we meet at the carriers?"

"Actually, my contact will meet us with the ship off the coast behind the island," Kaiden said and pointed to the south. "He wants to verify the pilot before we take off."

"I shall make myself as presentable as possible," Genos vowed.

"I think he's looking to grill you on specifics but that couldn't hurt."

"All right, it seems everything is set." Flynn pushed himself off the lamppost.

"Oh, do we have a name for this mission?" Indre asked.

Kaiden looked at Chiyo and shrugged. "I mean...no? This isn't an official mission or anything so there's no need to go through the all the annoying—"

"But it's fun!" she protested.

"It could add some flair," the marksman interjected. "But it wasn't like the merc gig we did a few months back had a mission name either."

"I suppose, for the sake of familiarity, we could call it something simple," Jaxon conceded.

"You're into the idea too, Jax?" Kaiden asked.

"Indre seems to enjoy the idea," the Tsuna pointed out. "It doesn't seem like such a big thing, and team morale is important."

"Fine, fine." He sighed and glanced at Chiyo. "I guess

since this all started with Chiyo's findings, and we'll be helping her old man, how about Operation Infiltration?"

She looked at him with surprise before it turned to amusement. "I suppose that is basic," she said with a small smile.

"That works for me," Indre said happily. "It makes it sound official."

"I guess it's better than Operation Fire Cobra Claw or something silly like that," Flynn admitted.

"If that is all agreed, I suggest we head to bed and be ready to go early in the morning," Jaxon stated.

"We shall be ready, Kin," Genos promised. "For the sake of friend Chiyo."

"It's cool to get to go on another mission," Indre added. "Especially since I can put the training I've had here to use this time."

"And you can actually prepare a little as well," Flynn noted.

Chiyo looked at the group. "Thank you, all of you."

"We'll get this done in no time and help you protect your pops," Kaiden said with a smile. "But I'm sure you weren't worried about that, right?"

She turned to look at him. "It would be foolish not to think of the potential complications and dangers as an infiltrator, and inconsiderate as a friend." She returned the smile. "But I was never worried about failing. I know who my friends are and what they can do."

CHAPTER FIFTEEN

Early the next morning, most of the group had arrived at their designated meeting place. Flynn yawned and leaned against one of the large trees in the forest. He glanced at Indre who appeared to be playing with something on the ground. "Are you doing some last minute modding over there?"

"Hmm? No, I found this." She turned and gestured to something and the marksman flinched.

"What the hell is that?" he yelped and stared at the container in her hand, which contained a grey insect with a long spike on the front.

"It appears to be an assassin bug," Genos interjected and crouched to look into the receptacle. "A rather rare specimen for the area, correct?"

"Yeah. I could probably get a few credits from a collector." Indre nodded and put the container away. "I'm kinda surprised you recognized it, Genos. Have you been studying bugs?"

He nodded as he straightened and looked around the

forest. "I find them interesting. We don't have anything that is an equivalent on Abisalo."

"There is that, but also the fact that they were a potential source of nutrients for us," Jaxon added.

"Really? It seems risky," she said thoughtfully. "We eat insects too, but they are natural to our planet."

"So are lobsters and crabs, but we can consume them fine," Genos pointed out.

She nodded. "Good point—oh! Speaking of cute things, do you wanna see the drones I'm bringing along?" She removed two circular drones from her bag.

"Those look like flying basketballs," Kaiden said as he and Chiyo entered the clearing. "Howdy."

"Good morning, friends," Genos responded cheerfully.

"Humph." Indre grunted and stowed the droids with puckered lips.

Flynn walked up to the duo and offered a handshake. "Good to see ya. It took you long enough to get here."

The ace took the marksman's hand "Sorry. We lost track of time getting the final preparations in order."

"As long as you weren't lazing about, I can't give you too much trouble." He chuckled. "So, when is Julio arriving? I want to see what rifle he has ready for me."

"He should be here any—" The air swirled and buffeted above them. Kaiden looked up and smiled. "Good timing."

"I didn't even hear it fly in," Jaxon shouted in surprise as the dropship descended gently and opened the landing gear seconds before it touched the ground.

"That's a nice ship." Indre whistled. "It looks like an Atmosphere Sail model."

"That's the base, but Julio has upgraded it over the last four years," Kaiden said.

"We used it during our previous operation. It will be perfect for this one as well." Chiyo placed a hand on his shoulder as she walked past. "Thank you for convincing him to let us use it again."

"Well, that all depends on Genos now, really." He sighed heavily and she froze momentarily. "He doesn't trust me to fly it for a prolonged period of time."

"I see." She looked at the Tsuna mechanist and shrugged. "It should be fine, then. He is both knowledge-able in aircraft and skilled as a pilot."

"I agree, but it depends on whether Julio agrees," Kaiden warned as the side door of the ship opened and a track unfolded from the ship door to the ground. The man in question stepped into view, dressed in a blue button-down shirt, white pants, and an ivory Panama hat.

"Hello and good morning, ladies and gents." He looked around. "I recognize you all from that night in the bar, so Kaiden hasn't scared you off yet. That's good."

"Nice to see you here so punctually, Julio." The ace shook his hand. "You're dressed kind of casual to be driving around in a stealth craft, aren't ya?"

He shrugged. "I've shuttered the bar for a while. I'll use this as an excuse for an overdue vacation. As soon as we're done here, I'll take the hyperloop to LA."

"It's good to know you'll catch sun while we fight for our lives," Flynn quipped.

"Are you really gonna grumble about something like that after nearly three years at Nexus?" Julio asked with a lazy smile. "You know that'll be your life for the foreseeable future, right?"

"Yeah, but some sympathy would be nice," the marksman retorted playfully and made his way to the ship. "Now, let's see what you got in there for—huh?" His march was stopped when the other man held a hand up.

"I can promise you I have the goods. I wouldn't have lived this long by being cheap with my clients—in both occupations." He lowered his hand and looked around, then pointed two fingers at Genos and Jaxon. "Let me speak to the pilot here. Judging from what Kaiden hinted, my guess would be it's one of you two gentlemen?"

Genos nodded and approached him. "Indeed, sir. I am Genos Aronnax, Master Engineer with four points in aircraft piloting and two for spacecraft."

"That's rather impressive, but piloting isn't even your main class, is it?" Julio inquired and stroked his chin thoughtfully.

"I am a mechanist, actually, although I have divided my studies into a number of fields to be as useful to my friends and future teammates as possible."

Julio nodded and slipped his hands into his pockets. "That's admirable. I was something of an engineer in my younger days. It's a fairly thankless skillset, though. It wasn't a choice between being a master or jack of all trades. You had to be both to get noticed."

Genos nodded in return and peered over the dealer's shoulder at the ship. "Speaking of which, elder Julio—"

"Elder?" He glanced at Kaiden who held up a hand to dissuade him from protest.

"It's respectful, trust me."

"Indeed, I hope I can address you as friend before long," the Tsuna added before he pointed behind him to the underside of the ship. "However, I wished to ask if that was the ship's balance drive?"

The man looked behind him. "Indeed it is. Nice, huh?"

"Quite nice, yes. It looks like considerable work has been put into it, so I wondered why it is deactivated."

The group looked at the device with shared confusion. "Deactivated? That's because the ship is powered down isn't it?" Flynn offered.

Genos folded his hands behind him. "When a ship powers down, most devices will normally do so with it. But a drive like that will actually remain on, albeit in a power-saving mode. Starting it from a completely deactivated state will require more prep time before takeoff and readjustments after that. I would have assumed that it was some kind of mod or additional power core attachment that would allow it to completely power down for some other reason, but it deactivated before the rest of the ship and immediately before landing. "

Julio blinked a few times in surprise before he grinned, then laughed and withdrew a chip from his pants pocket. "Well done, Genos. I had actually planned to make it be part of the test for you to look the ship over to see if anything was off, but you saw it even before I could ask."

"Does that mean he's worthy or something?" Kaiden asked.

"It means he knows his stuff, at least the basics," The dealer handed Genos the chip. "Let's take a deeper look. We'll go to the cockpit and go over the pilot's chair."

"Can we go onboard as well?" Chiyo asked.

He turned and shrugged. "I guess I can't say no. I have a good feeling about this pilot. That's no surprise, really. The Tsuna were spacefaring before we were." He clapped the mechanist on the back. "I have cases of equipment in the bay for all of you—part of the deal. You guys go through them while Genos and I have a closer look at my pride and joy."

"Awesome. Let's head on, Indre," Flynn shouted and raced past Julio and onto the ship. She followed quickly.

Jaxon walked up beside Genos. "I'll see you after you're done, kin. Make sure to go over everything in detail."

"Of course. That is how I do everything," Genos promised. "I'm sure you're about to do the same. You seem as excited as friend Flynn."

The Tsuna ace stiffened and didn't reply as he went up the track into the ship.

"That's his version of excitement?" Kaiden asked as Chiyo bowed to Julio and boarded the ship herself.

"You couldn't tell?" Genos asked and tapped his infuser.

"He's…difficult to read, even after all this time," he admitted.

The mechanist nodded. "I suppose I can see that."

"You made a good choice, Kaiden," Julio stated and hung his other hand over the ace's shoulder. "Maybe my standards have lowered with all the gunheads I've dealt with in the last few years who don't appreciate a good ship, but I like this engineer's potential."

"You are rather happy. Are you drunk this early in the morning?" he snarked as the three entered the ship.

"Not yet. I'll make a start on that as soon as I step foot onto the hyperloop. Do you really think I'd fly my baby if I had so much as an allergy headache, much less if I was drunk?"

Kaiden had to relent. The man made a good point. "So we have the ship. Where's this package you wanted me to take and who will receive it?"

"It's in the bay with the equipment. I collected your stuff from that armory you had it stored at and took the initiative to restock your explosives and make some fixes, free of charge."

"That's rather nice of you."

"You're good for business. I've been given more gigs to deal because of your track record. A better list of accomplishments means people look to deal through me, which means I get a better cut," he explained as they entered the craft. "Keep it up and I'll invite you to a barbecue some time for gold-star clients."

"I'm sure I'll get there in no time," Kaiden promised and took his leave. "I'll get suited up. Make sure we get up in the air ASAP, Genos!"

"Certainly. Let's go and take a look, elder Julio," Genos stated and headed into the cockpit.

Julio sighed and waved at Kaiden. "I'm trusting you, both with this ship and to come back in one piece, got it?"

"Of course!" the ace said and gave him a thumbs-up.

The man returned the favor and moved to catch up to the mechanist. "Hey, I know it's a nice thing and all, but you can drop the whole 'elder' thing, kid."

"Of course, elder Julio."

He shook his head with a lazy grin. "I... Come on, man, let's go over the board."

CHAPTER SIXTEEN

"Do you like the rifle, Flynn?" Indre smiled. It really was a rhetorical question as the marksman had examined the weapon for the last half-hour.

"Hmm? Oh, hell yes. Take a look." He set the safety switch and handed it across the bench to the agent, who immediately cracked it open to check the energy unit.

"So this isn't a kinetic model like the one we used at the Ramses gig?"

He smiled, opened a compartment on his leg, and slid a cartridge out. "It's actually the best of both worlds. If I press that switch, it shuts the core off and engages the kinetic version. In fact, the lining can activate the—"

She snapped the gun shut and tossed it back. "It's really cool, but I don't need to know the details." She drew her pistol, a rather small model. "As an agent, I have so many gadgets that I have to use in a variety of situations, I prefer my weapon to do only one job—shoot."

Flynn folded the rifle and placed it beside him on the

bench. "Fair enough, but it doesn't look like that little cricket can do much damage."

"That's why I have to get in close," she clarified and aimed it briefly at him. He immediately held his hands up. "But there's a mod here that increases the punching power. It still won't let me do as much damage, but if we do have to have a full-on firefight, I can still support the others without putting myself in a vulnerable position."

"You do not have a primary weapon?" Jaxon asked as he completed the inspection of his own machine gun and pistol.

"I prefer to use the extra room for gadgets," she stated and gestured to a cylindrical pack on the back of her suit.

"I can agree with you on that." Chiyo entered the bay. "Speaking of which, can I get your help with one of mine, Indre?"

"Sure, what do you have?"

The infiltrator retrieved the box Laurie had given her and handed it to her teammate. Indre opened it and beamed. "Man, I haven't seen a Genesis system like this."

"Genesis system?" Flynn inquired and frowned at the silver crescent-shaped device.

Chiyo nodded. "It's a condensed operations system with a cyber suite that allows for similar technological integration as our technician's suite, but it's run by either an installed EI or our personal one if it's up to the task."

"*I am on standby, madame,*" Kaitō offered.

"Thank you, Kaitō, but I need to understand exactly what we're dealing with. This is actually a model designed by Professor Laurie himself."

"Really? That's awesome. How did you get it from him?"

the other girl asked and tried to turn the device on.

"He wanted to…help out," she said. "Also for field testing. I worked through everything, but if I can find the right mode and get the connection system working correctly, I can give a drive to Kaiden. He can simply use that to get the information we need instead of him sneaking back. I thought having two technicians looking into it would be more productive than one."

"I certainly agree." Indre stood quickly, her expression eager. "There's a little table in the back—it's darker over there too and better for the holoscreen."

"Much obliged." Chiyo thanked her as the two walked off. Kaiden entered as they left.

"What'd I miss?" he asked and zipped his coat.

"Girl talk…I think?" Flynn responded.

"That looks like the outfit you wear in the Animus," Jaxon noted.

"The armor is more normal gig armor, but the coat is based on it, though," he confirmed as he took a seat. "I need to be more stylish. Vox has its share of bounty hunters, mercs, and all that, along with security, so guys walking around in armor isn't abnormal. But still, they are watched fairly closely so I'll need to be sure I attract as little attention as possible."

"You said that part of your agreement with Julio for the ship was to make a delivery. How long do you think that will take?" the Tsuna ace asked.

"Hopefully, no more than an hour. The bay we'll land at isn't too far from my rendezvous point. After that, I'll hunt for the agency that has the neurotech device we're looking for."

"Is it something big?" Flynn asked and leaned back. "Do you need help carrying it there?"

"I thought it might be, but not so much, as it turns out." Kaiden slid a hand into his coat pocket and withdrew a small black cube that wasn't much bigger than his hand.

His companions regarded it curiously. "What the hell is that?" the Aussie asked.

"I have no clue. One of my rules is not to ask about it." He tossed it to Flynn, who caught it and scrutinized it. "He didn't say nothing about you guys, but I assume he thought about that."

"Where do you even open it?" the marksman asked as he turned the cube over. "I see some notches...maybe it requires a key of sorts or it's locked with a voice code." He lobbed it to Jaxon, who simply looked at it.

"I would guess that it either has data that requires a specific device to access or it's a phantom box," he stated.

"One of those containers that nukes the thing inside unless you open it the right way?" Flynn frowned. "We'd best not mess with it, then. If it is a phantom box and we fry it, I assume that effectively cancels the deal."

"Good idea." Kaiden put his hand out and Jaxon returned the box. "I can't imagine what would be so small and valuable without it being precious jewels or something. Maybe it's a hand-off," he suggested and slipped it carefully into his coat.

"Or something else illicit," the Aussie added. "Julio's a nice guy, certainly, but you don't make it as far as he has without having to deal with unsavory customers on a regular basis."

"He has his own code of ethics. I don't think it's something we have to worry about," the ace said casually. "It doesn't mean I won't potentially be getting wrapped up in something, but I'm only the messenger."

"One who can kill instead of the opposite," Jaxon pointed out.

"Sure enough, and I imagine he counted on that too, But like I said, I hope to wrap it up quickly so we can get the real job done and move on to the main objective."

"Chiyo's father, right? The head of Mirai," Flynn looked thoughtful as he considered what he knew about the company. "All the big corps in Australia and New Zealand use their stuff—not only cybersecurity and hardware, but they have an offshoot art house for design work. My Uncle Jensen's company actually had one of their office's logo and interior designed by them."

"She hasn't spoken much about her family or her past in general," the Tsuna stated and glanced at Kaiden. "I don't want to overstep my bounds, but I assume there is a reason."

"It's somewhat muddled, that's all I'll say. I probably already said too much when I filled you in earlier," he admitted. "But she's still concerned enough that she wanted to do something if she could. It all depends on what we find. If the truth be told, this could be something bigger than I would usually guess a mission like this would lead to."

"Someone with the power and smarts to try to take over a world-renowned Zaibatsu would already be big, don't you think?" Flynn asked.

"Maybe it's more power than smarts," Jaxon countered. "Then again, I'm not sure what we can offer here. I have no doubt in our abilities, but what can we do compared to Mirai's funds and connections? If Chiyo has already informed them, haven't they begun looking into it?"

Kaiden leaned over and nodded. "They have. A few of her old mentors still work there and one of them is in charge of the investigation. Apparently, they've made more direct moves as well as their roundabout method. They caught a guy trying to sneak into one of their labs."

"That ain't smart. They must have him locked up somewhere?" Flynn asked.

"For a while, they did," he replied.

"He broke out? That's rather crafty."

He shook his head. "No, when they went interrogate him, all they found in his cell was his clothes and some goo."

The Tsuna cocked his head and Flynn winced. "Goo? Did he melt or something? I'm sure they have camera feed."

"They had video, but it was looped after he was put into holding. They didn't see what happened. According to the police files Chiyo was able to gather, the same thing happened to the guys she and I intercepted a couple of nights ago."

The marksman shivered. "That's unsettling."

"Was it some kind of suicide device? In case they were captured?" Jaxon inquired.

"Probably, or their insides were set to melt after a certain time," Kaiden answered with a shrug.

"That's not helping," Flynn grumbled.

"I'm not being facetious," Kaiden retorted. "They are called golems—basically, human skin suits that can be controlled with the right hardware. Laurie told me about them."

"Paratechs?" The three looked up when Indre and Chiyo returned.

"Close. It's the same idea," he confirmed. "I don't know if we'll run into more but keep a lookout. I don't want you losing your lunch when you have a good look."

"I'd prefer to run into one of them over a neurosik, honestly." Chiyo shuddered and Indre grimaced with distaste. "Do you think that's possible?"

"We're flying by the seat of our pants here, but I've heard of merc companies and terrorist cells using them in the past," he warned.

"Greetings, friends!" Genos called over the comms. "I'm sorry for the earlier delay and rough ride. I had to make the proper readjustments after eld—friend Julio removed the balance drive chip. We're only six minutes away from our destination and have clearance to land."

"It looks like we're about to actually start the mission." Flynn beamed and hoisted his sniper rifle as he stood. He attached it onto the magnetized strips on his back. "All right, Kaiden, what are we doing?"

The ace stood and stretched. "I have a delivery to make, then I'll go for the device."

"Yeah, right, right. We know that, mate." Flynn rolled his eyes. "But what are we doing?"

He looked at his teammate as he picked a case up with one hand and slid his other into his coat pocket. "You? You're tourists."

CHAPTER SEVENTEEN

"Welcome, ladies and gentlemen, to tonight's ArenaMAX festivities," a rather exuberant man announced over the arena's speakers.

"You know, I would normally be more excited about something like this," Flynn muttered and pulled his helmet on. "Getting to run around and show an adoring crowd my skills? I'm not above a little theatrical fun."

"And yet I feel as if you are rather saddened, friend Flynn," Genos commented and examined his personal cannon.

"We came here on a mission, yeah?" the marksman questioned and closed the locker door. "And now, we simply have to goof around?"

"We're needed for the next part. Chiyo and Kaiden have got this one," Indre reminded him. "Besides, think about this as a warmup."

"A smart observation," Jaxon agreed and holstered his pistol. "This is more than a game. Not only does it give us an opportunity to test this equipment, but we also have an excuse to wear it. If anything does go down, we will be ready to support them."

"All right, MAX fans. Let's get ready for the next round. Will team seven please come to the arena entrance."

"Is that us?" Flynn asked.

Genos shook his head. "We are team eight, the next one up."

"Each round is only fifteen minutes. We'll be up soon," Indre said encouragingly.

"All right." The Aussie leaned against the locker. "So what's the objective here? We collect enough tickets to get the fancy hoverboard on the top rack?"

"You're in a mood right now," the agent teased as she stood. "There are prizes, but the top four teams out of eight move on to the next round. The top two from that round face off after that, so we'll be here a couple of hours at least."

"Unless Kaiden calls us," Jaxon reminded them. "Although he hoped they would be finished by the time we are done."

"So we'll play the full round, then?" Flynn stretched his arms. "Well, I'd better stop moping, I suppose." He took his rifle out and checked the core. "We don't get to use kinetic rounds but firing lasers in an enclosed area with civilians seems rather risky."

"There's a shield guarding the stands. That would be the main reason we aren't allowed to use kinetic rounds," Genos clarified.

"You have to give it to the guys who made this place," Indre commented. "Vox gets a large amount of traffic from bounty hunters and mercs. Having a place like this where they can make use of their skills and make a real profit was very smart."

Jaxon nodded. "It also keeps them in check by letting them blow off steam here instead of in some bar."

"Although, considering the one we passed on the way here, that doesn't seem to work one hundred percent of the time," Genos said, rather bemused.

There was a knock on their door. "Pardon me." A woman walked in wearing a red jumpsuit with the ArenaMAX logo and gestured at the group. "You'll be up soon. It doesn't look like team seven will last the whole round."

"Really? It's only been a few minutes," Indre responded with surprise.

Jaxon let a small smile form. "So this might actually be a challenge, then."

"Oh, we know our clientele," the woman said with a smirk. "There's no point in inviting veterans to simply do some glorified target practice."

"That's good to know." Flynn shouldered his rifle. "Where to?"

"I'll lead you to the entrance when you guys are ready," she informed them. "Also, I wanted to thank you for showing up. It's off-season for the pro teams, and it's the down season for all the merc traffic we usually have. We were worried we wouldn't have a full roster of teams."

"I'm glad we could help," Jaxon replied. "A friend of ours suggested this and it seemed like it would make for a fun evening."

"I suppose everyone has their own definition of fun." She shrugged. "The fans are sure to love it. We have over ninety percent capacity filled so put on a good show, all right?"

"No worries there, missy," Flynn promised with a clenched fist. "We'll win this and get Kaiden the giant stuffed bear as a memento."

The woman blinked and glanced at the others. "What's he talking about?" Indre simply sighed and tapped the side of her helmet in annoyance.

"Have you made the delivery yet, Kaiden?" Chiyo asked over the comm link.

Kaiden finished chewing a bite of the kebab he had bought from a street vendor. "I'm almost there. I needed to make a quick stop."

"I noticed you went down one of the commercial streets," she muttered. "Also, I can hear the sizzling over the speakers."

He took another bite. "Give me a break. I didn't get to have more than a power bar for breakfast. I gotta keep my strength up."

"Good point. Fetch me something on your way over," she ordered.

The ace swallowed and rolled his eyes. "Couldn't you have used a word other than 'fetch?'"

"It seems appropriate, actually," Chief quipped.

"I need to go dark. I've approached the agency and I want to lower the chances they can track me as much as possible. I'll see you soon." Her line cut with a muted click.

"And she avoids a response," Kaiden muttered as he turned a corner and headed into an alley.

"According to the directions, this should lead directly to the recipient," the EI informed him.

The ace retrieved the cube and flipped it a couple of times. "This was rather straight forward. Are you sure no one followed us?"

"Positive. No one tailed us. But there's always the chance they could be waiting for you up ahead or this is a trap."

"I don't see anyone here, although that could be something to worry about as well," he replied thoughtfully. "I don't think Julio would knowingly send me into a trap, but there's a chance this is a test of some kind."

"What do you think is in the box? Maybe a kidney?"

"That would be a small-ass kidney." He chuckled and examined it again. "Maybe I've simply assumed the worse. But you get a little paranoid when someone specifically tells you not to ask what is in the box."

"Hey, we're here."

Kaiden peered down the alley that still stretched far ahead but paused when he saw a glowing arrow pointing toward the left. He grimaced and turned his attention to a surprisingly ornate door above five stone steps.

"I know I said I'd get used to it, but you could have simply told me it was on my left," he griped as he jogged up the steps and knocked on the door.

At first, he received no response. No one called a reply and he couldn't hear any movement within. Maybe he arrived when they weren't home? Was this a home or an office? When the door slid open slowly, it caught him by surprise. A woman with long blonde hair that curled at the ends stood in the entrance. She had kind green eyes and wore a flowing white dress.

"Hello, young man, how can I help you?" she asked, her voice almost sing-song.

"This is the last person I would have imagined we were delivering to," Chief said, flabbergasted.

"No kiddin'," Kaiden muttered under his breath. He straightened and adjusted his coat. "Hello, I'm Kaiden. I'm here to deliver something on behalf of Julio Salazar."

For only a brief moment, he could have sworn he saw the woman twitch, although it might have been the chill in the air. "I see. May I have it?"

"Certainly, it's why I'm here." He held the box out and she took it and studied it for a moment before she raised her other hand. She wore a bracelet with six different objects attached to it. Her expression calm and smiling, she removed the jewelry and held one of the objects to the top of the cube. It flashed green when the object made contact and the top folded open in four sections. She looked inside and her smile slid from her face to be replaced by one of contentment. After she'd examined the contents for a moment, she nodded and placed the box on a table near the door.

She looked at Kaiden and her soft smile returned. "Do you mind waiting here? I need to send something in return."

That wasn't part of the deal, he thought but he shrugged and nodded. He had to return the ship at the end anyway.

"I'll only be a moment." The woman turned and walked away to disappear around the corner.

He leaned against the railing of the stairway and rolled his neck from side to side, more out of boredom than anything else. "Well, that was simple enough."

"She left the box open. It's right there," Chief pointed out. *"Do you wanna take a peek?"*

"I was raised better than that," he retorted.

"Bull."

The ace smiled. "Honestly, I think it's simply that what I thought it might be is actually cooler than whatever it really is. Considering what she looks like, it's probably a gift for one of Juli—"

"I'm back." The woman stepped around the corner.

Kaiden straightened and turned toward her. "All right, what do you need me to—" A loud and ominous crack preceded a violent pain in his chest. The force catapulted him from the door, and he rolled down the stairs and landed hard on the pavement. His instincts kicked in and he shoved onto his knees, drew Debonair, and aimed at the woman. "What the hell, lady?"

"I see that Julio is smart enough to send someone in armor, at least. Even if he's still a coward," she sneered and lowered her hand cannon. "Tell him this makes up for his last mistake, but if he's late again, I'll come personally,"

The ace lowered his pistol, confusion written on his face. She reached for the door handle. "And as for what I need to be delivered, that shot was meant for him. Where you put it is up to you." She slammed the door closed. Kaiden stood and his hand actually shook a little as he holstered his pistol.

"Hey, Chief…" he began, then grimaced and clenched his teeth for a moment. "Get Julio on the comms."

CHAPTER EIGHTEEN

"And that was team seven, eliminated in only seven minutes. Kind of fitting, huh?" the announcer declared and tried to make a joke of the situation, but it didn't really settle the booing.

"All right, let's forget about them and move on."

"That crowd out there are rather bloodthirsty, aren't they?" Indre scowled.

"Well, if you're a regular spectator here, I'd imagine you've seen some good matches up to this point," Flynn pointed out. "That team didn't even last half the match time, and I think they only scored a couple of thousand points."

"Eighteen hundred," their attendant informed them. "I think that's technically the third lowest score ever at ArenaMAX. Although we've had over twenty teams get zero, so that's a multiple tie."

"I guess they can hold onto that for a silver lining." The marksman snickered.

"How much time will they need to ready the field?" Jaxon asked.

She looked wryly at him and brushed at a streak of dust on her staff uniform. "Not long at all, I'd imagine. You might as well step closer to the gate and take a look at the field."

Genos was already in place and stared at the clean-up below. "It's a fairly level field with a few pillars and large obstacles for cover, three watchtowers, and two large platforms on either side." He looked at the group. "The robots seem to be typical battle models—Guardians, Soldiers, and the like. I assume each type is worth their own set of points?"

"Spot on." The attendant nodded. "I guess I should have given you guys the full overview. I got a little caught up in the preparations."

"It's cool. We had a rundown of the rules before we went into the locker room," Indre replied. "Our friend is merely cautious."

Flynn approached the gate and studied one of the towers. "Will we stick together or do our own thing?"

"I suppose I'm open to either," Jaxon responded with a shrug.

"You guys seem confident," the attendant stated and clasped her hands behind her head. "But like I said, we make sure these are tough. Our visitors want a challenge and we wouldn't have the ravenous fans we do if we pulled punches."

"And yet I can see that the droids don't use top-of-the-line power cores for their energy weapons," Genos said. Flynn leaned forward as the Tsuna pointed to where a pile of parts was being taken away by a Cleaning droid. "I assumed that was a cost-cutting measure at first, but those tubes are meant to fortify the joints in a droid's body. It adds extra defense but at the expense of movement and snap targeting, which is one of the reasons you would want droids for battle instead of organic soldiers."

"So a big part of the challenge, then, simply comes from the fact that they might be a little harder to destroy than normal," Indre summarized.

The attendant blinked and scratched the side of her cheek a little sheepishly. "It's not like it was a big secret or anything, but I have to say you have a good eye there, sir."

Genos turned and gave a quick bow. "Thank you. My discipline is engineering, for the most part."

"Team eight, I hope you're ready," the announcer cried.

"It looks like you guys are up," the woman declared with an excited clap. "Best of luck. When you're done, come back through here and I'll be ready to congratulate you."

"See you in about fifteen minutes, then." Indre skipped beside Flynn and Genos with Jaxon behind her.

"So, free-for-all, then?" the marksman asked.

"They are essentially slower versions of the droids we've trained with for the last three years," Genos reminded the team.

Jaxon cocked his head and stared over the field. "Be sure to tell the others if you need help."

Flynn laughed. "Are you really worried?"

The Tsuna ace shook his head. "Not about you getting hurt, no." He began to walk through the gate. "But we will have individual scores as well as a team score. I wouldn't want you to fall too far behind me."

The Aussie was honestly taken aback by the boast. Genos tapped his infuser and looked at him. "You know, he's talked to Kaiden much more these last few months."

His teammate laughed again. "Yeah, I can tell." He hefted his rifle. "And I doubt I can get under his skin as easily with a few playground insults, so I guess I'll have to put some work in."

The people on Layton street cleared a path as he strode forward. Some tried simply to get home quickly, while others wanted to finish their shopping before the evening rush. However, a good number wanted to avoid the man who spoke loudly into the comms in his ear, even though most people didn't see a device.

"She shot me because you're an asshole," Kaiden snapped and fixed his gaze on a point in the distance. The crowds parted automatically to give him space.

"Do you know that for sure? Maybe she was an assassin?" Julio suggested. The ploy wasn't helped by his barely contained laughter.

"And how is that better exactly?" he retorted and turned down another street. Many of the shoppers breathed a sigh of relief as he walked away. "That means you knowingly sent me to an assassin's doorstep."

"You're acting like that's a big deal. What have they taught you at that academy?" the other man asked.

"Restraint, fortunately."

"So you did pay attention in those discussions. I'll tell Chiyo you willingly ignored her."

"Shut it, Chief."

"Yeah, yeah, take it out on me."

"Seriously, Kaiden, do you think I would knowingly send you into a dangerous situation?" Julio asked. His tone was still jovial, but a hint of seriousness showed through. "Fair enough, I guess I do that as a job. But I wouldn't trick you like that, especially not after the Brazil gig."

Kaiden stopped in the street and sighed heavily. "Are you still beating yourself up about that?" he asked, and a little tension slid away in favor of a calmer tone. "Don't worry about it anymore, Julio. That's the past now." His tone became a little more agitated. "Especially when the present annoys me far more."

"Yeah, I get that from the vibes, and I'm hundreds of miles away." The dealer chuckled and ice cubes clinked against glass. "Look, in all seriousness, Marie and I have something of a…complex relationship."

"If this is leading to a sex confession, you can stop now."

Julio snorted. "It wasn't, but a quick word of advice. Before acts of passion, don't eat any spicy peppers. It's apparently an uncomfortable sensation for the fairer sex."

He rubbed his temples and grimaced. "Dammit, man."

"Solid advice, though."

"And how would you know?"

"Experience," the dealer related.

"I wasn't talking to you." The ace rolled his eyes. "In any case, I assume you did something to piss her off. And I have evidence to back me up if you try to weasel your way out of that." He looked down and slipped a finger into the hole over his left breastplate where he had been shot.

"Yeah, but I didn't think it would lead to her attempting murder," Julio muttered. "Last time I saw her, she only tried to tase me."

"Well, it's certainly escalated since then," Kaiden retorted.

A series of rather high-pitched giggles issued from the usually deep-voiced Julio. "I'll make a mental note to send her good wine and the macrons she likes so much from a dessert boutique in Seattle. That should work as a peace offering."

"Make sure the delivery man rings the bell and runs." He glanced at a map of the city and confirmed that he was about ten blocks away from the agency. "I guess this has been a rather long way to confirm that I've made your delivery. I have to take care of my main objective now."

"I see." Julio sipped noisily. "I'll not ask too many questions about that, then."

"That's probably smart."

"Seriously, though, Kaiden. Thanks for completing that little errand. Best of luck to you."

He smiled. "I appreciate it, Julio. Once we get the device and decide what we have to do from there, I'll call you and let you know when we'll get your ship back to you."

"Take your time. I expected this to be at least a week," the man responded. "But make sure to come back as intact as my ship."

"No worries there. Dying isn't one of my talents." He chuckled.

"I would hope not, considering you can only make use of it once. Take care, Kaiden."

"You too, Julio." He ended the call.

"You know, you've gotten soft over these last couple years. Our spats from the first year were way more intense."

"To be fair, I can't get too mad at the guy who keeps giving me work," Kaiden admitted. "Still, it was a dick move."

"We're close to the agency. Should we give Chiyo a call?"

"Nah, I'm sure if something came up, she would call us." The ace looked around. "Although thanks for saying something. I forgot to get her something to eat."

"I saw a takoyaki stand back on that other street. Do you think she would like that?"

"Maybe. That's Japanese right?" He thought about it for a moment. "Maybe I shouldn't make assumptions. But she didn't specify."

"That kabob you got is about twelve blocks back."

"To hell with that. Let's get the squid balls and hope those will suffice."

"Such enthusiasm."

CHAPTER NINETEEN

One shot and three droids in a line are dead. Flynn smirked. He looked at the board, sure that he should have enough points to keep Jaxon humble.

Team Eight - 38,450 points

Jaxon – 11,600 points
Genos – 9,750 points
Indre – 8,800 points
Flynn – 8,300 points

Time Remaining: 7:42

What the actual hell? He was last? It could only be because he took the time for clean kills. The others simply raced around and used the old spray and pray technique. The marksman drew a deep breath to ease his irritation. He shouldn't rag on his teammates because he knew they were good, and this kind of match was where their strengths lay. Although he was partially right, he would need a change in tactics if he wanted to catch up. He saw mechanicals from the corner of his eye, adjusted his sniper rifle casually, and fired two shots with a simple pivot to blow both their heads off. He holstered his weapon and retrieved his sub-machine gun before he leapt off the edge of the watchtower.

Genos spun from the cover of the large stone and fired a concentrated blast. It annihilated two of the pursuing droids, but the Guardian still stood, although not for long. Most of its front plating was compromised. He drew his hand cannon quickly and fired two shots. They connected, demolished the droid's power unit, and deactivated it. More of the enemy approached, both Assault and Soldier, and he needed distance and a way to group them. He had been hit a couple of times—fortunately not enough to damage his armor, but his shield needed a little more time before it would be back at one hundred percent.

The Tsuna kept that in mind. They still had a mission to complete and it would be a waste to damage his armor in play, even in a situation that might be considered too violent to be merely a game. This was the same reason he didn't use any of his explosives or gadgets at the moment. There were a few restocks on the ship, but that would be a misuse of inventory.

A flurry of activity from the Assault droids released a volley of lasers toward him. He rolled away from the attack and scrambled across the field to one of the pillars. Once behind cover, he adjusted the funnel of his cannon. It didn't look like they would group together, but he could probably obliterate them with a beam sweep.

He spun to fire, but the enemy teetered and fell, all shot in the back by a drone that hovered behind them. In the distance, Indre waved at him. She apparently didn't share his concerns about using gadgets, but she was an agent and could repair the drone if it was destroyed.

He couldn't say that about a thermal grenade.

Jaxon snatched the arm of the Assault droid and sliced into the shoulder joint, then reached in and ripped out the exposed circuits. The arm began to spin wildly, and he kicked the mechanical away as a Soldier droid rounded the corner and was immediately felled when the first collided with it. The malfunctioning arm smashed into the head of the new arrival and the ace pounded his boot into the head of the Assault droid. It was all a little reckless, certainly, but he had gained the lead and had yet to see anything but Assault, Soldier, and Guardian droids.

These presented no real challenge, so he had to make his own. He hadn't had the opportunity to practice his blade skills recently and this would do. Something shattered rock and he whirled to identify the cause—a Brute droid with a cannon on one arm and a dense frame that protected its body. It couldn't move quickly, but the cannon caused area damage and if he was caught by its free hand, it could easily lead to shattered bones. He couldn't recall the last time he'd fought against one during training.

It raised its weapon and prepared to fire. Jaxon almost drew his pistol, but he saw no other droids around. He might as well keep to his own rules for now. Even if it took him a couple of minutes, this one might be worth the points. It should prove an interesting experience, at least.

"Those four are from Nexus Academy?" a man in the spectators' booth asked.

"According to the files, yes," his teammate replied, looking at a holoscreen. "They are all third years—Masters as they call them."

"Masters?" a brutish man responded with a chuckle. "Hell, that's a four-year school, isn't it? What are the fourth years called?"

"Masters, at least until they graduate. Then they are Victors."

"Good Lord, that's pretentious." The bigger man laughed and took a swig of beer.

"Says the oaf who calls himself Lycan." A woman sighed as she placed the newly cleaned scope back onto her rifle. "And pretentious or not, they could beat our score by the end of their time."

"We didn't take it seriously," Lycan responded. "At least I didn't. And Lycan is only a code name."

"That you demand we call you," the hacker retorted. "Then again, Fred doesn't exactly strike terror into anyone."

"You got that right." He laughed and finished his beer. "It looks like they will be the ones we face in the finals."

"I agree," their leader said with a nod. "Unless there is an upset in the next match, they seem to be the most competent."

"It'll be good practice," the woman commented and peered down her scope. "Our targets are from Nexus, right?"

"Yeah, but that doesn't mean they are all the same," the hacker countered. "If it was that easy, the Academy would have been closed down long ago for how many failures they pump out. If everyone fought the same way, once you learn the trick, it's over."

She nodded. "Still, the training has to be topnotch. To see a group in action will give us some median for their ability at least."

"They are fun to watch in action," Lycan admitted and cracked another beer. "The last six matches were all bores. These guys at least aren't all huddled together and turtling across the field like team four."

"I've only paid half-attention," the hacker admitted. "Still, do you think it's related? These guys being here and our upcoming gig?"

"I would say it's a hell of a coincidence otherwise," Lycan grunted and shifted in his seat for a better look at the field below. "Think about it. We've been here a few times. Have you seen a group of academy students make field trips here?"

"Either way, it's not our concern for now," the leader pointed out and drew the attention of the other three. "We don't know all the details or the pay, but we got a million credits simply to hear the potential employer out. For now, observe them. If we can gather any information, we can use that to increase the payout and as a potential advantage."

His companions exchanged looks before Lycan shrugged and put the beer can to his lips. "Fair enough. There's no use jumping the gun. If we did happen to find this Kaiden guy or Chiyo girl and took them out here without knowing the full scope of the job, we could potentially lose money or the gig. They might say we already killed them so why pay for a job we didn't take?"

"That's why I hate the secretive types," the hacker complained.

"That's ironic, coming from you," the sniper pointed out.

"Time is more valuable to me at this point than money," he stated and closed the holoscreen. "That employer wanted a meet-up, probably to make a spectacle to convince us to take the gig."

"Hey, now. A spectacle usually means a free meal," Lycan stated with a wide grin. "The fancy stuff too. I can't say that's not worth the trip."

"Can you really not buy your own filet mignon?" the hacker muttered.

"Of course I can." The other man huffed, crushed the beer can, and tossed it into the trash bin across the room. "But it always tastes better when someone else pays for it, and those rich guys always have connections to the really good stuff."

The hacker shrugged, withdrew a pack of cinnamon gum from his jacket pocket, and peeled the silver coating away. "Either way, if this is an assassination job and we had the chance to do it here and spare us hours or potentially days…" He popped the gum into his mouth and started chewing. "I'll be seriously annoyed."

"A truly frightening prospect," the sniper muttered sarcastically. She looked at one of the screens. "A minute and a half left, and they have already passed our score by three hundred points."

"Impressive," the leader conceded. "This arena isn't exactly a challenge to those with real skill, but I like the fact that they still take it seriously. It shows spirit."

"Same here," Lycan declared and pounded a fist into the couch.

"Great, he's already drunk," the hacker complained and blew a bubble with his gum.

His teammate glared at him. "I drank a six-pack. What kind of lightweight do you think I am?"

The hacker peered across the table at another box. "These cans have an ABV of six percent each."

Lycan shrugged. "And your point is? I'm simply excited. The last three times we came here, we steamrolled to a win. This time, it might actually be fun."

"And yet this is always your suggestion when we come into port," the sniper commented, leaned her rifle against the side of the couch, and sat in the adjacent chair.

"You won't let me get into bar fights anymore," the man retorted and leaned back in the couch.

The leader chuckled and the hacker sighed and threw his hands up. "You're hopeless."

"And that is it," the announcer cried. "With a final score of

84,900, team eight are the overall winners of the first match."

Flynn glanced at the final scores.

1. *Jaxon – 25,600*
2. *Flynn – 20,200*
3. *Genos - 19,900*
4. *Indre – 19,200*

He sighed but his smile was still a little satisfied. It was close between him, Genos, and Indre and he was happy that he had been able to climb to number two. But damn, if Jaxon still didn't have a hefty lead. He had to admit that like Kaiden, the ace could back his talk up with action.

He merely hated to think what it would mean to have two Kaidens running around.

CHAPTER TWENTY

Chiyo deactivated the Genesis and had a clear point of entry to her destination. She looked across the rooftops to the agency five blocks away. The sun had begun to set and they would have to move before too long. Assuming Kaiden arrived relatively soon, they could start just after dusk.

She felt something poke at her back and spun as she reached for her blade. Kaiden held a box in an outstretched arm.

"Howdy," he said cheerfully and popped a fried ball of some kind into his mouth "I brought you some food."

"I...uh...oh." She moved her hand from the hilt of her blade and put the Genesis device away as well. "Thank you. I suppose I should have been more aware of my surroundings."

"Chief said you had several traps and trip wires set up even a couple blocks back." He handed her the container. "I think you were more than enough prepared, but I know what to look for by now."

She accepted the box with a nod. "I forget how percep-tive you are at times."

"It's more how I've learned to be." He took a few steps past her and studied the scene. "Is that the agency? The silver building with the blue top?"

"Yes. Fortunately, since we got here so quickly, they haven't moved the neurotech device to a warehouse or down to earth yet." She opened the takeaway and a familiar scent drifted from it. "Takoyaki?"

"Yeah, and it's good too." He held a skewer up with two of the four takoyaki balls already finished before he removed another and popped it in his mouth.

Her meal contained four skewers and a couple of cups with different sauces. "You should try this sauce with the last one," she recommended and showed him a dark-colored sauce.

Kaiden turned. "Really? It looked like Worcestershire sauce and as I'm not a big fan, I didn't bother."

She tossed him the cup. "It's similar to that but not as intense—takoyaki sauce, made specifically to be paired with takoyaki, obviously."

He shrugged, opened the lid, and moved the last of his takoyaki to the top of his skewer before he dipped it. "So, now that you've had a look, how do you think this should go?"

"Honestly, you may not like it," she admitted, opened the Japanese mayo, and dipped one of the snacks into it.

"Why's that?" he asked before he ate the last ball. He raised his eyebrows, impressed at the taste. "That is good."

"I'm glad you liked it." He handed the cup back to her before they both looked at the agency in the distance.

"There isn't much room to maneuver in there, certainly if we want to avoid being detected, but I found a way to access the device without having to sneak it out."

"I thought we already knew that. We were simply gonna use that Genesis device to download everything on it, right?"

"We were and still can, but that's plan b now. I believe I can access it remotely if I'm close enough." She tapped the device on her hip. "It can send a signal, briefly activate the device as if it connected to another mind, and in that time frame, I can get what we need."

"Cool. I'm enjoying this rather laidback start, to be honest. It's a pleasant change of pace." He ran a hand down his coat and hovered over the hole. "For the most part, anyway."

"You were shot?" Chiyo asked and noticed the mark for the first time.

"Yeah, but I'm all right. Better than Julio might have been," he grumbled. "Or he might have been all right too. The dude's good at sweet talking. I only want to break a finger or something now instead of stab him."

"That's deescalating to you?" she inquired.

"Yeah...I was shot," he said and picked his teeth with the skewer. "That's damn near generous, really."

"I suppose." She sighed, finished one of her skewers, and picked up the second one, then blew on it briefly to cool it.

Kaiden looked over the edge at a trashcan on the street. He flicked the skewer casually into the air. The wind carried it to the receptacle and it hit the rim and fell in.

"Anyway, this sounds good. So what's the part I'm supposed to hate?"

She walked up beside him and pointed to the agency with her skewer. "I have to be close for the signal to reach. It looks like I can stand beside the building or out front, but there's a risk that someone will get suspicious. I shouldn't need more than a few minutes since I can simply download the data and look at it on the ship, but I'm sure the police would be on edge if someone hovered around the agency, especially after what happened."

"Good point. So I assume you need me to cause a diversion or get their attention?" he asked.

"Yes, and I have a suggestion for that," she answered and indicated a building nearby. "There's a bar there, one that has a reputation for brawls. The cops usually patrol nearby because of it."

He grinned. "It'll need to be a big brawl to really get their attention."

"I think it's well established that mayhem is your forte," she reminded him.

The ace nodded. "Oh, that won't be a problem. Getting out of there without being caught up in it myself might be the tricky part, but I'll manage."

"Then if we're agreed, we'll move soon. The rush should start within the next twenty to thirty minutes," she stated.

Kaiden nodded. She was on her final takoyaki skewer. "Wow, you went through those quickly."

She chuckled and bit into another ball. "Takoyaki is one of my favorite foods, actually. I usually have to go into town to get some when we're at the Academy."

His smirk was a little smug. "Really? I'm glad I chose them, then."

"It was my suggestion, though," Chief reminded him.

He shrugged and nodded. "Good call," he muttered under his breath.

"Either way, it probably meant more coming from you."

"You think so?"

"Yep. I don't even have to give you a readout. Take a look."

The ace was puzzled but another glowing arrow pointed him toward Chiyo. She smiled as the sunset illuminated her in silhouette and certainly seemed happy and even serene in that moment.

For once, he didn't think of the action ahead and allowed himself to simply enjoy a peaceful interlude.

"Sir, there was an accident. Have you seen the new reports?" Rei asked as she entered the room and composed herself quickly. "I'm sorry for barging in, sir."

"It's all right," Gendo said, his eyes focused on the screens in front of him. "And I'm looking through all of them now. It seems something is afoot—more so than we thought."

"All those people…" she stammered. "Who would…how could they?"

"Strategically, no one would link the Urahara group to us. We weren't officially involved or partnered with them," he stated as if he rattled off stock market information. "They must have discovered the projects we kicked to them. I can't tell if they looked for those projects or hoped they would have more information on us that they could exploit."

Rei was shaking. Whoever had broken in, they had no problem causing a scene, even if it was one that no one would find until later. "Maybe it was simply a break-in that turned violent?"

"That is doubtful," he responded dryly as he dragged one screen across and enlarged it. "If it was merely ruffians looking to make quick cash, I doubt going to a business district with guard patrols and advanced security was a wise move. Even the most spontaneous or irrational thugs would pause at that, and the area wasn't close to any areas with high crime rates. This seemed flawlessly planned and executed."

She walked up beside her employer and winced at the photos onscreen. "Executed... That's appropriate."

"You are correct with at least one facet of this, Rei," he said curtly as he leaned back in his chair and adjusted his glasses. "They aren't being subtle anymore. They could have made this look like a crime for profit or left evidence to point to some other reason for their presence. But they targeted the group that worked on our projects. This is a message as well as an assault."

"What kind of message, sir?" she asked. "That they will target us next?"

"I doubt they would escalate that quickly. They would have to know this would immediately put us on the defensive and that we'd plan for an attack like this." He stood and strode to the window and the view of Tokyo, his hands clasped behind him. "I believe they know we will watch for whoever they are. They want to show us what they are willing to do to accomplish whatever their goals are and that if we don't acquiesce to them, more will suffer because of our inaction." He sighed and turned back. "This isn't the first time something like this has happened. It's a common fear tactic."

Rei observed her boss. He seemed calm and collected and simply considered the issue in his head as if it were a mathematic equation that needed to be solved. It seemed rather cold, considering the loss of life, but she could see that something troubled him.

"Still, I am worried," he stated and paused for a moment. "While it's clear they are after us in some way, I have no idea why."

CHAPTER TWENTY-ONE

"Well, that was pointless." Indre scowled at the scoreboard.

Team 8: 101,600 points
Team 6: 49,200 points

"No kidding. We have more than double their points." Flynn yawned and stretched with his rifle across his back. "Did we get a bad group or is off-season merely this off?"

"The other team seemed rather young," Jaxon noted and gazed across the arena floor at the other team, whose members sulked as they retreated into the opposite tunnel. "Perhaps they are apprentice mercenaries or something like that. Maybe they were here to see where they stand currently."

"If that's the case, I hope we didn't discourage them too much," Genos replied. "They had good form and didn't take too much damage. They have potential."

"It could have been an amateur team or something," Indre suggested. "This is actually a sport with pro teams and all that."

"They definitely need more practice, then." Flynn watched the screen as it called for teams one and four to approach the arena. "I guess we'll see who we'll be up against at the end of this. Who wants to head back to the locker room? I could use a juice."

Genos looked at Jaxon and nodded. "That sounds good. They have screens in there so we can still watch."

As they turned to leave, their assistant waved at them and shouted congratulations. Jaxon paused for a moment to study team one when they emerged from the western entrance. All wore helmets except for the large one in front, who had wild long hair and a feral grin and pounded his fists together in excitement. They had the highest score before he and his team had taken the lead—but only by a few thousand —and even from this distance, they seemed different than the other teams he had watched and played against.

He wanted a good challenge. It would be a good test of skills, but something seemed off about them. It had something to do with the way they carried themselves, even the cocky one in front. There was form and a deliberation to it, not the impression of a team of people looking for a good time or even a simple perception of strength. They carried the air of professionals who knew their skills and abilities and hadn't seen anything to put them on edge.

The ace frowned, a little uneasy at the instinct that warned him that he and the others would need to be more alert than ever.

Dario sipped the coffee in his cup and scowled at the screen in annoyance. It had taken far longer to peruse this information than he had hoped. If he had known that he would spend the rest of his night twiddling his thumbs, he would have taken longer at the Urahara building than he did.

But Yvette insisted that they wrap it up quickly. She was certainly skilled, took orders well, and worked fast—maybe too fast. Perhaps she should learn to enjoy the experience. He glanced back to see her cleaning her weapons. She'd been rather quiet since the night he'd picked her up. Eventually, he would have to make good on his promise to help her spring her former leader. He wondered if that would cause an issue in power balance. The EX-10 were a team made up of traitors, after all.

"Are we done for the evening?" she asked and snapped him out of his thoughts. She stood. "If so, I'll retire for the evening."

He smiled and ran a hand through his hair as he returned his attention to the screen, which confirmed it was sixty-seven percent complete. "This thing has a while to go, then I'll ship it off to have it examined. No more work for now." He stood, walked up behind her, and reaching into a cabinet above them. "Have you eaten yet?"

"I have a stock of replenishment bars. I'll be fine until we're done," she answered.

"We're at a rather nice hotel and the kitchen is run by a celebrity chef of some kind." He took out a bottle of wine and closed the cabinet. "I'll order room service. Would you care to join me for dinner?"

"I'm fine," she responded, picked her weapons up, and walked away. "Thank you for the offer." With that, she disappeared into her room and shut the door.

He frowned as he located a corkscrew. "Pity. I suppose all work and no play is only a concern if you know how to play in the first place." He uncorked the bottle and wandered away to find a glass, then took a moment to look out the window. "This really is a nice city. I should come back here when I have the time."

Settled into Yvette's former seat, he poured wine into the glass, kicked his feet up, and perused a menu. "I should probably enjoy this time. I don't think I'll have another opportunity to enjoy myself like this for the next few days."

"Sir, you have an incoming call," his EI announced.

Dario sighed, set the menu down, and retrieved his EI pad. "Okay, let's see who— Ah!" He smiled and answered. "Merrick, good of you to call."

"Dario, a good evening to you," he replied, and his hologram nodded. "How goes the mission?"

"So far, slowly." He sighed and took a sip. "We acquired what information we could from Urahara, but we already knew most of it. There are a few promising leads and one or two things we can use, but unless the scan finds anything else, the bodies we left are more important than what we found."

"So you have begun to look through it?" his boss asked.

"Oh, certainly, even before we got back into the room." He nodded. "I actually intended to call you once I sent everything over."

"I see. What will you do from here?" the leader asked.

"I've considered a couple of different plans," he said casually. "One is a little slower, but I think we can wear them down through intimidation and attrition. The other is…rougher, but you would see results much faster."

Merrick looked cautiously at his friend. "I have no problem with you handling this as you see fit. However, you do remember one of the few rules I gave you, correct?"

Dario smiled. He knew exactly what he referred to. "Of course I remember. Don't kill Gendo. But there's considerable leeway in that order, you know. I assume you know me well enough that you would have been more specific if you were worried about excessive damage as well?"

For a moment, the other man glared at him, but he didn't flinch or react, at least physically. Still, he noted that his friend didn't seem to be in a playful mood tonight. Merrick composed himself and shook his head. "You would be right, but I specified that the reason I didn't want him dead in the first place is because we would still need him for official purposes and as a potential public face. I know you like finding loopholes, but you are smart enough to know that it's hard to convince the public that everything is fine if he's suddenly missing appendages."

"It's nice that you believe in me." Dario hummed and took another sip. "If you don't have a preference, I suppose I'll choose, but tell me something." He cocked his head and regarded his boss curiously. "Has Gendo's daughter made a move?"

Merrick nodded. "Not only her. She appears to be working to track us using her own means. She has assistance from Kaiden and a few of her compatriots from Nexus."

"A real go-getter, she is." He looked out at the Tokyo skyline. "I suppose we should consider that there is a chance they could find a way to muck this up for us. What is the worst-case scenario?"

"That they do something to stop our acquisition of Mirai and reveal us to the world at large."

"Oh, that is grim." He sighed. "I might have to adapt my second plan and be more forceful—within reason of course." He stroked his chin thoughtfully. "Do you happen to know where they are?"

"They went back to Vox. I assume it's to acquire the neurotech device," Merrick explained.

"You haven't recovered it yet?"

The man's hologram glanced aside as if reading something off-screen. "We should have it soon, but they could get what they need before we reach it."

"Merrick, tell me truthfully, do we need to get the Mirai company right now?"

The leader looked back at him, concern on his face. "Hmm? I thought you were ready to take it?"

Dario put his glass down. "Even the faster of the two options would take some time, and if they get that device, you know where that would lead them."

His boss closed his eyes and he opened his mouth to speak, then closed it again and thought deeply. "You believe that if they do find their way there it would be more troublesome than potentially losing Mirai?"

"We haven't come so far in the acquisition that we can't

afford a diversion," the assistant reasoned. "Right now, they only know that someone seems to be after them but can only guess who it might be and what we're truly trying to achieve. We can still set some things in place and pull the curtain later. But if that girl finds us, that would lead to all kinds of problems, wouldn't it?"

Merrick grimaced but nodded. "It certainly would, but we are well prepared. Do you think it would become a problem you need to handle personally?" He glared at Dario once more. "Tell me, Dario, are you trying to intercept them simply because you're interested in fighting Kaiden yourself?"

He smiled. "Admittedly, I have an interest. He has proven to be much more troublesome than we thought. It was also my responsibility to recover the EI, and I've obviously failed at that."

"I thought you referred to it as a work in progress," the other man countered but his gaze softened slightly.

"One that's been in progress for three years now," he stated and refilled his glass. "I think that if I use my time to prepare for them—to take care of them—I can kill several birds at once. I could take care of Kaiden and take the EI implant, and we would have the girl as a hostage."

"Hostage?" Merrick inquired. "That's not usually your style."

"I'm willing to bend my personal rules for your sake," he explained. "It would make up for the time I would have lost by my change in priorities."

The other man looked off-screen again, then leaned back. "I will...agree that I see benefits at least. If you're willing to accept the consequences, I'll take over on the current mission for you while you head to the facility."

Dario almost shattered the stem of his glass in his excitement. "That's very kind of you, sir. Although before I get ahead of myself, I suppose I should wait to see if they actually get the device. You'll know soon?"

"I will, and I will let you know as soon as I do."

He stood and checked the screen, which now read seventy-nine percent. "The scan is closer to completion. I'll send it to you and the techs as soon as it's finished."

"Understood." Merrick reached over to turn off his device but paused for a moment to look at Dario. "Take care, my friend."

The assistant nodded. "Don't worry so much, and I'll make sure to bring you some souvenirs along with either the implant or Mirai."

"See that you do." He signed off.

Dario downed his glass in one long drink and hardly took the time to enjoy its flavor. His night had improved considerably now. He sat, leaned back, and stared at the ceiling. Vox was it? He believed the merc group he'd made contact with was there. Maybe he should simply give them the details now? He dropped the idea immediately. No, he would pass them over to Nolan. If this did require his personal touch, he wouldn't pass up the opportunity.

He flipped the glass idly in his hand as his mind raced. There was a lot to do and plan if they did discover the facility. He would have to identify who else was with Kaiden and Chiyo and ensure the damage didn't get too out of hand. In addition, he'd need to plan to cover their tracks. Otherwise, eliminating them would simply lead to more suspicion if they told anyone then simply disappeared.

Humanity first, that was their motto and that was the mission. It really was ironic that he took such pleasure in the kill considering all that.

CHAPTER TWENTY-TWO

Kaiden walked into Populi, the bar Chiyo had pointed out to him. It had a metallic layout with neon lights and glowstrips used in place of traditional lights. The rest was a traditional bar set-up with booths and bar chairs like they originally designed it to be a night-club and changed their minds halfway through. Still, it was reasonably pleasant, all things considered.

And unfortunately for him, that seemed to extend to the clientele. Most seemed happy to chat amongst themselves or watch some kind of arena match on the holo-screens. It didn't seem like he would be able to pass the buck to some punk to create a ruckus this time.

He'd barely accepted the thought when he was shoved from behind and managed to catch himself before it became a problem. As he glanced over his shoulder, a skinny man with shaved white hair and dyed lines streaked across it give him a greasy smile and moved past him. Several others followed and either gave him the stink-eye or more condescending sneers.

They all walked to a circular booth in the corner. Their leader ran his hand over a couple of women's necks, who immediately yelled at him, but he simply waved them off with a laugh. Kaiden watched them as a smile crept onto his lips. He didn't have to ask Chief about the chances of this working out anymore.

Casually, he approached the bar, retrieved his credit chip, and placed it on the counter.

"What'll you have?" the barkeep asked but his glance strayed continually to the new arrivals as well.

"Are you worried about those freaks?" Kaiden asked and gestured a thumb behind him to point at the punks.

The man's gaze darted between him and them. "It all depends on how they're feeling. They always order a hell of a lot of booze and pay for it as well. It's the only reason I let them keep coming."

"They've tried to start stuff before," the large man beside him added as he drained his beer. "Although they always back down. I would love to throw their asses out a final time, but Jim won't let me until they actually do something."

Well, that wouldn't do. "So they're all talk, then?" He settled on a barstool and spun to face the man. "Are you the bouncer?"

"I bodyguard," he answered as the barkeep refilled his glass. "But I'm also a regular. I keep telling Jim here to let me help with the riffraff and make this place more relaxed so folks don't have to deal with all the fights that break out."

"You keep saying it's part of your workout routine now," Jim, replied and slid a full glass to the bodyguard.

He smiled and raised it. "It doesn't mean I wouldn't mind some R and R on occasion. In fact, simply taking out the trash would actually be therapy considering the stuff I usually get into."

"You should let Rok take 'em, Jim," the man next to the bodyguard interjected. "Felix and I will even help out. That should minimize the damage—right, Felix?" he asked and nudged the man on his left, who simply shrugged and downed some of his beer.

"Are you guys bodyguards too?" Kaiden inquired. He examined them casually as the gears in his head began to turn faster and faster.

"Yeah. Kruger, Felix, and I all belong to the same company." Rok replied and took a slow sip. "Damage is one thing. If it was only that, I would do the deed myself, but there are always unknown players. Like those mercs in the far corner."

The ace had noticed them too. Four of them wore medium armor and they didn't have weapons on them. Either they had left them behind like he had, or they must have been locked up at the door. They seemed to keep to themselves so he had written them off, but if a fight did break out, they might be drunk enough to join in.

"But if you help out, kid, that might even the odds," Rok suggested and grinned when Kaiden gave him a puzzled look. "Don't try to play coy. Even if I didn't see the top of your armor under that jacket, it's almost armor itself if you take a good look at it."

Kaiden chuckled. "Fair enough. I actually only wanted a quick drink, but I have a history of dealing with bastards like that, particularly in bar settings."

"Now hold on a minute, all of you." Jim grunted and regarded the four with a stern expression. "I appreciate the gesture. You're trying to help, even if it's in your own meathead way, but you three are some of my best customers. You won't do me any good if you're locked up for a couple of weeks." He pointed at the ace. "And I haven't seen you around here before. With that armor, I guess you're here to relax between gigs? How would you rate a place that immediately roped you into a fight?"

He shrugged. "Well, I haven't had a drink yet, but I would give four stars based on the entertainment alone."

Rok and Kruger chuckled. Felix downed his drink and flipped his empty glass onto the coaster.

"Why do I always get the hotheads?" Jim muttered caustically. "Besides, like you said, they haven't done anything yet. There's no use knocking around a bunch of—"

"Hey, are you gonna serve us, you old bastard?" one of the punks shouted. The ace looked over his shoulder. Three of the seven slouched at the table, their expressions irate. Two others flirted with women close to them, and the last two snickered at some shared joke. His gaze darted to the other side of the room. The mercs scowled amongst themselves and one seemed to actually tremble with annoyance.

He'd worked with less, he decided and looked at the barkeep. "I understand. I won't do anything to them, sir," he promised.

Jim sighed. "As much as I'd like to make an example of these guys, it's not good to—"

Kaiden spun in his chair. "As for you three..." He picked his credit chip up. "How much for your services?"

Chiyo had waited for the promised diversion for about twenty minutes. She studied some of the buildings around the agency, although it wasn't exactly a great cover as there wasn't much to look at—mostly business centers, a tailor's shop, and a shooting range. Noise had flared from the bar more than once and each time, she had hoped it was the start of his distraction. Unfortunately, it usually died down as quickly as it started. She wondered irritably how much longer it would take.

Banging, yells, and worried shouts erupted. That wasn't easily mistaken. She glanced at the bar as she retrieved the device. A body catapulted out and a man in a leather jacket, bruised and with blood dripping from his nose, tried to crawl to his feet before another man landed on top of him. This seemed to be the start. She glanced at the agency when three men rushed out, their attention focused on the bar. One pointed and they ran off as a couple of others looked over from the top of the stairs leading to the entrance.

Is was a dust up, for sure, but it would need to be much more before it really drew anyone's attention. As the three officers reached the entrance, they were shoved back by two mercenaries who erupted through the doorway in a struggle with two other men. A larger man stormed out with another beside him and several civilians shouted and screamed as they ran out after them. The mercs saw the cops, thrust their opponents aside, and began to argue with the officers when they ordered their surrender. The miscreants cursed volubly and gestured obscenely in a challenge for them to fight. The two officers still in the agency yelled to someone inside and went to assist, followed by several more.

Chiyo seized the opportunity and raced across the street, activated the Genesis device, and slunk into the alley next to the agency. She brought up her connection to the systems and scrolled down her list of commands to activate the start-up signal. It triggered and launched the neurotech device within. She would need a few minutes. If she tried to do this haphazardly, it could alert the technicians who watched for infiltrators like her.

Although hearing what was going on down the street, there was a good chance Kaiden had given her all the time she needed.

"Technically, I'm not doing anything," Kaiden pointed out and sipped his lager.

"You did start it." Jim winced as a body careened past behind the ace.

"The bodyguards are only doing their duty. You can't blame a man for putting in good work."

"I'll kill everyone in this bar," one of the punks shouted before Felix beat him across the head, snatched him by the neck of his jacket, and tossed him across the room.

Kaiden took another sip. "Besides, you don't seem that pissed."

"Call it desensitized." The man sighed and began to clean the bodyguards' glasses.

"I'll leave a good tip. I have the creds to spare," he

promised before he took a moment to think. "Although I'm racking up the expenses lately. If I'm not careful, I could end up spending more than what my contract would have been worth."

"Contract?" the barkeep inquired with a curious expression.

The ace grinned and looked at his glass. "I'll have a refill. And add a request for you to not mention that if anyone asks."

"Twenty creds for the refill, and keeping a secret is market price." He chuckled and took the glass.

He sighed. Rok and a merc exchanged blows while another punk attempted to make a crude Molotov cocktail. He stretched forward to snatch a glass and whipped it behind him. It shattered in the man's face and he yelled when glass shards embedded into his skin. Both Rok and the merc spun and kicked him.

"Add it all to the tab," he stated and took his refilled glass from Jim. "That glass too."

CHAPTER TWENTY-THREE

Team 1: 138,700
Team 3: 50,600

"That's a new top score for the semi-final, MAX fans!"

"Damn," Flynn muttered as he stared at the final tally. "They beat our score for sure."

"I would say that team three was certainly more skilled than the team we faced," Genos noted. "And even then, this team one... They are far superior. Are we sure they are only here for fun?"

"You could make the same argument about us, really," Indre pointed out.

The marksman leapt up from the bench. "So we have our opponents then." He retrieved his rifle and powered it on. "Should we head over to the entrance?"

"You're certainly fired up now," Indre teased. She stretched her arms and placed her drone back into its compartment. "Although I have to admit, I'm a little excited myself. This looks like it will be fun."

Genos walked over to Jaxon, who continued to stare at the screen. "Kin, do they seem quite proficient to you?"

"Do you mean for a team of people simply here to blow off steam? Or are you comparing them to us?" the Tsuna ace asked, his attention still focused on the screen.

The largest member of the team waved to the cheering crowd. "It's rather strange to say, but outside of the Animus, I think they might be the most skilled opponents I've had to face." He tapped his infuser thoughtfully. "It's odd to run into them in a playful situation such as this."

"You weren't there for the EX-10, though, Genos," Flynn reminded him as he walked over to them with Indre. "Those guys seem good, but I doubt they can measure up to wanted killers like those we faced. Right, Jax?"

Jaxon picked his helmet up from the table in front of him and put it on. "I suppose we'll have to see."

Flynn and Indre looked at each other. "Wait—what, mate? It's up to debate?"

"It's a possibility," the ace reasoned and faced the group. "The next match will be a challenge between the two top teams. According to the rules, killing is illegal, but I doubt that would stop them if they felt like it."

"Well, this suddenly got real," Indre whispered to Flynn, who nodded.

"I can't imagine they would unless one of you has a history with them that I don't know about." Jaxon's expression remained calm.

The trio shook their heads. "I can't say I've ever seen them before." Flynn shrugged. "They are all wearing helmets so it's hard to tell, but I would have remembered that shaved sasquatch-looking guy."

"Are you referring to the cryptid from the past or the mutant?" Genos asked.

"Same difference, really."

The door opened and the assistant poked her head into the room. "Are you guys ready? Team one wants to get started right away."

Chiyo heard footsteps and moved one hand instinctively toward her pistol as she glanced up. She relaxed when Kaiden strolled down the alley, his coat flapping behind him.

"Did you get everything?" he asked.

"How did you get away?" She turned the device off and placed it on her belt.

"I was only a patron, technically. I was more impressed that the guys I hired got away. They can move like bunnies despite being as big as houses." He grinned and looked at the device, then at her.

She nodded. "I have it. Let's rendezvous with the others and we can go through it and continue from there."

Kaiden offered a hand. "It would probably look better to walk out of here as if we were simply a curious couple," he reasoned but hesitated, a wary expression on his face. "Then again, they might be more worried about the fire."

Chiyo looked up and frowned at the faint trace of smoke beyond the entrance to the alley. "There's a fire?"

He grimaced. "It just started. I thought I stopped the guy who tried to start it but maybe one of his buddies picked up where he left off. Although it's not in the bar. He tripped and threw it at a building across the street."

"It seems things got out of control, even for you." She chuckled and took his hand.

"I didn't exactly try to control the chaos in this case," he admitted as they left the alley and sauntered down the street. She paused to look back at the carnage. "It did spiral a little, I gotta say. I guess we should head over to the arena."

"Do you think they are done yet?" she asked and squinted ahead at the dome in the distance.

"They should be on the final match unless things ran long," he replied and checked the time on his HUD. "We can send a message for them to forfeit."

Chiyo thought it over. "I...I wouldn't want to ruin it for them, even if we are running on a tight schedule."

"Flynn threw a fit when I sent them there," he recalled. "They might not mind."

"We'll see how far they are when we get there," she decided. "They deserve a little fun before the action if they can get it."

"Someone, get this bastard off me!" Flynn shouted as Lycan almost caved his head when he stamped his massive foot. He managed to roll away barely in time.

"Your legs still work, right?" Indre shouted as she dodged blasts fired from her own drones. "One of them hacked my babies."

Genos hammered a shield spike into the ground. It activated and shielded him and Jaxon against two more sniper shots fired from the other side of the arena. "They are indeed persistent."

"Can I see your cannon?" the ace asked, and his teammate handed it to him. "Break away and take shelter over at that pillar." He pointed to the south. "See if you can get around them and use one of your nano grenades on the hacker to shut him down."

"Understood." He took one out and primed it. "I had hoped to avoid using too many gadgets."

"And it was a wise move, but we need all the advantages we can get right now," Jaxon held the trigger down. "This team are professionals, and not only in this competition. They move and fight like the EX-10, but their skills seem to be even more considerable." Their shield shattered from a thermal blast and he nodded to his teammate, who raced away while he ran to intercept Lycan who still harried Flynn.

"Flynn, take care of the sniper!" he ordered and fired the cannon blast at the feet of the giant. The merc shielded his eyes and jumped back as it erupted, landed smoothly, and looked at Jaxon with a broad smile.

"You look like you can put up a fight," he challenged and pounded a fist against his chest. Now that he could see it more clearly, the ace realized it wasn't heavy armor, but light.

"You're not a titan?" he asked.

"A what now?" Lycan balked before he snapped his finger and grinned. "Ah, right. You're one of those Ark academy guys and have official classes and terms and all that."

The Tsuna began to charge another shot. "How did you know that?"

His opponent smiled. "I can tell by how you fight. You have talent that's been refined. It's either that or you apprenticed under a general or something."

"I trained with warriors in my clan before I ever stepped foot on Earth." He aimed casually. "Although I doubt it takes much training to realize a large target like you should wear heavy armor." He fired but Lycan simply moved his shoulder back and the orb sailed past him and erupted against the shield that protected the audience. The explosion drew both frightened and excited shouts. Jaxon's eyes widened in shock.

"My training was in battle. Hell, I was born in it. It's a fun story." The large man drew a hand from behind his back. He'd slipped a metallic gauntlet on with several tubes that ran from the back of the hand. When he activated it, small jets of smoke poured out and the metal around the fingers began to glow. "If you are conscious by the end of this, I'll tell you about it."

Genos ran from cover to cover. The team's leader and marksman had both targeted him and his left shoulder plate had been damaged by a sniper shot. Thankfully, he managed to evade the latest attempts and slid behind one of the rocks, drew his launch pistol, and placed the nano grenade inside. He had a good idea where the hacker was. The man didn't seem to be moving much, but he had yet to take any damage. It seemed safe to assume he had some kind of shield or barrier protecting him. He wondered if he would have to waste two grenades, one to get rid of the shield and the other to turn off whatever device he used to control Indre's drones.

There was also the risk of him controlling the nanos. He shouldn't have the time to do it, but if it took too long for them to eat through the shield, it might buy him the time he needed and would make the situation worse. Another sniper shot whistled ominously. Genos waited for the impact, but none came. It didn't even strike his cover. Two more shots were fired, but each sounded different. He peeked around and saw Flynn targeting the sniper in the split second before the leader almost took his head off with machine gun fire. The Tsuna dragged in a breath, relieved at his narrow escape. He needed to get away or the man would be able to take him at his leisure.

He placed a finger against his helmet. "Friend Indre, do you have any EMP missiles?"

"Yeah, I have. One sec—dammit. He got my arm," she muttered over the link. "I have one left. I already tried to take out the hacking prick, but he was able to deactivate it before it hit."

"I think he might have a barrier as well," Genos added. "The leader is focused on me, friend Flynn is busy with the sniper, and kin Jaxon is dealing with the larger one." He frowned at his launcher. "I have a nano grenade ready, but I might have to use two or more and I don't think I have many left on the ship."

"We are taking this seriously, huh?" she commented wryly. "I've got it. You only have to use the one. I'll give you an opening here in a sec. Use it on the leader."

"What about the hacker?"

"You know how to throw a punch, right?"

Jalloh was impressed with this group, or at least with how long they'd lasted. He had to commend their abilities as well. They gave Lycan and Cascina a good fight. He looked at Raz, who had yet to move from the spot where he'd started. He didn't seem to be enjoying himself like the others were.

A blast careened past his head. He hadn't even heard anyone come from behind. He spun and fired at the opposition team's agent, who had obviously shaken off the hacked drones. It was a direct strike, but she continued her approach. He smiled slightly when he realized she was a hologram. It was a good trick. Something battered against his back and he realized immediately that this was not a trick. His helmet, chest, and weapon were enveloped by hundreds of small orbs. In seconds, his weapon deactivated, and his armor began to unlatch—nanos. He moved quickly to activate a switch on his belt that covered him in a red light. The nanos began to drop off. He turned to see the mechanist had run off and now headed directly toward Raz. His teammate would have to move now.

The Tsuna lunged forward as Raz noticed his approach and fumbled for his pistol. He pounded his fist into the side of his helmet and drove him out of his protective sphere. Jalloh almost laughed at that. The simplest solutions were often the best, it seemed. He drew his pistol and fired at the two drones before the agent could gain control of them again.

"You bastard," she yelled and aimed her pistol at him. "Do you know how long it'll take me to repair those?"

"Someone of your caliber? A couple of hours at most with the parts ready," he replied and aimed his gun at her. "Laser burns take a bit longer, however."

"Agreed." She fired and he raised his hand, activated his reflector, and bounced the shots back. Two caught her in the stomach and one in the chest and she fell heavily.

"I didn't say I would make them." He chuckled and holstered his pistol.

"I'm not done yet," she threatened and scrambled to her feet.

"Perhaps not." He turned and walked to the edge of the arena. "But this match is."

An alarm went off. Indre, Genos, and Flynn looked up in surprise.

"That's time, ladies and gentlemen," the announcer shouted. *"And with a score of one – zero, team one wins."*

"They scored?" Flynn shouted and glared as the rival sniper walked away.

Indre and Genos walked over and Jalloh helped Raz to his feet "When? Who?" Flynn demanded fretfully.

"Hey." The trio turned toward Lycan who smiled and held Jaxon by his helmet. Most of the ace's armor was shattered and broken. "He was a good fighter. Make sure he recovers so we can have a rematch, all right?"

He dropped the Tsuna's semi-conscious body. Indre and Genos surged forward to catch him and help him up. Flynn scowled as the huge man walked away and waved to the crowd once more. Jaxon was one of the best fighters in their group, and all he saw was scuffs on his opponent's armor.

Who the hell were these guys?

CHAPTER TWENTY-FOUR

"How's he doing?" Kaiden asked as he made his way into the ship.

"I'm up, Kaiden." Jaxon sighed and moved the ice pack from his jaw to the top of his head. "I know this is a traditional remedy for soreness on Earth, but it makes my muscles numb."

"That is the idea, mate," Flynn explained from the repairs desk. "Although how numb are we talking? It sounds like you're talking with a mouthful of cotton."

"I can't move half my jaw," the Tsuna muttered and rubbed a hand gingerly over his face.

"We are a little more sensitive to extreme cold," Genos interjected as he checked on his kin and took the pack from him.

"Is that right?" Kaiden leaned against the wall. "It's a good thing you didn't come along with us to that outing in Alaska that Wolfson took us on."

"We didn't exactly come along either, Kaiden," Flynn retorted. "You know, I still go into a cold sweat around the end of the year, waiting to be dragged away to some unknown location for another gladiatorial match."

"And yet it seemed like you had a good time at that ArenaMAX place."

"I was coming around to it, until that last match." The marksman motioned to Jaxon. "He had a bad feeling about them. I didn't take it that seriously considering how much of a cakewalk it was up until then. But those guys… Man, they were something else."

The ace looked at the group. "Do you think they were pros?"

"It would seem so." Genos nodded and handed a tube of some kind of serum to his fellow Tsuna. "I know that professional is only a title to signify status. But these people were… Professional professionals is all I can think of."

"I follow, I think." He looked out the window at the night sky that drifted by. "We left in a hurry, but Chiyo is still looking for our next destination. Are we simply flying in circles Genos?"

"I set the autopilot to head toward Tokyo," the mechanist answered. "Chiyo's father is located there, correct?"

"He is." The men looked up as Chiyo and Indre entered from the back room. "But that's not where we need to go now."

"Really?" Kaiden straightened, his expression a little confused. "So where do we need to go, and why exactly?"

"We weren't able to find any information on their plans for the Mirai zaibatsu," she replied and held the Genesis device up.

"But what we did find was a unique signal code," Indre

added. "My guess is that it was the connection between the neurotech and whoever he was transmitting to."

"And it leads to a facility in Germany," the infiltrator finished.

"Germany, huh?" Kaiden said thoughtfully. "It's a pity I don't speak it. I'm actually part German."

"You do realize that translators are standard for even commercial EIs, right?"

"Thanks for the fun fact," Kaiden retorted. "So, the fatherland. What's there and how should we approach?"

Chiyo walked into the center of the group, placed the Genesis device on the floor, and activated it. A hologram of a factory appeared in the air. "It would appear that this is the factory where the neurotech and his friends were sent from—maybe a headquarters?"

"So we'll go to get more info?" Flynn asked.

"If we can get some, I would certainly take it," she agreed. "But I'm concerned about it taking too long."

"Taking too long?" the ace questioned and glanced quickly at the others. "Now I'm concerned because that bothers you. You usually prefer the taking too long approach."

He expected a smart retort but instead, she simply looked down. "I received a message from Rei, my father's assistant. A group of people was murdered. They were a team that worked on projects for my father. The police were called in by the morning group when they arrived."

Flynn and Kaiden's fists balled, and Jaxon stood and placed his hand on her shoulder. "So whoever is after them, they seem to have escalated their tactics."

She nodded. "They don't know if it is simply intimidation or whether they were looking for something in partic-ular and wanted to get rid of witnesses."

"Probably both," Kaiden surmised. "The assailants obvi-ously had the time to move the bodies if they wanted to. The disappearances would have eventually caused an investigation, but it wouldn't have been so blatant as to who the target was."

"This shouldn't change the plans though, right?" Flynn asked. "I know we've played it by ear up until now, but if we have a destination, we can at least go there to start, can't we?"

"You are correct, but my fear is..." Chiyo's voice wavered and she looked at Kaiden.

"That this could lead to some kind of attack on the company proper?" he hypothesized.

Jaxon stepped away from her, sat on the bench, and leaned over with his hands clasped in front of him. "We originally worked on the suspicion that they were trying to take control of the Mirai zaibatsu. In a forceful takeover like that, they would have the entirety of the city against them, at the very least. And you said that the Mirai has connections with the WC. This would seem like a very foolish plan on the part of the conspirators."

"I don't think they would be that bold," the infiltrator reasoned. "But there are other ways to force a takeover, including a few that would at least appear legal if the right actions were taken."

Kaiden turned to Genos and gestured to the cockpit. The engineer nodded and left. "We'll head there now. There's no need to waste time speculating if we stop them."

"I'm not sure we can. We still don't have a clear target,"

she reminded them. "However, if we can at least divert their attention away from Mirai, we can buy time until more is uncovered. If we are able to smoke them out, that would put many more eyes on them. With my father's significant resources and connections, he would have no trouble amassing a force to deal with them."

"I'm sure he's working on things at his end. Whatever else might be an issue for him, he hasn't climbed to the top by being weak-willed or idiotic." The ace held onto a railing as Genos banked the ship. "We need to slow them down and I think we can accomplish that. After all, no factory means no production."

"We certainly have other factories available, but it would still be a shame if we lost this one. And it doesn't take a lot of information gathering to know that Kaiden seems to like his missions messy." Dario cut another piece of cake and popped it into his mouth. "My, this is delightful."

"So, I'll have another shot at him, then?" Yvette asked and strapped her armor on.

"I'll handle the boy myself. I've yet to have a proper 'shot' at him myself, you see." He swirled the wine in his glass before he took a sip. "He intrigues me."

"I have a vendetta." She hissed angrily and glared at him.

"You have a boyfriend locked in prison. And once this mission is over. I'll assist you to break him out, on my honor," he promised.

Yvette moved her hand to her blade. "He's my leader.

He—forget it. Have your fun. But you'd better keep your promise. You've only coasted on it until now."

"My dear, you've seen me work. You're the spirited kind, and if you thought you could actually force me to obey your whims, you would have done it by now." He tapped his fork against the plate. "Besides, that Tsuna is with him. He's the one who helped to apprehend your friend, isn't that right? I'll need him dealt with along with all the others he's brought along. But leave Kaiden to me and leave Gendo's daughter alive."

She turned to head to the cockpit. "Understood."

Dario took another bite and looked above him. The translucent ceiling of his ship revealed the stars hurtling past as they flew to the facility. "How long until we land?"

"One hour and twenty minutes, sir."

"More than enough time to finish my dessert, then," he noted happily. "I wonder if I should prepare a grand entrance of some kind for our meeting."

CHAPTER TWENTY-FIVE

Chiyo studied the data she'd recovered from the neurotech device. There wasn't much, however. She and Indre had combed through every detail, but she had hoped there was something she'd missed. Better yet, that it would be something that could lead to whoever worked behind the scenes and formulated this plot—something that would banish the feeling of doubt that had plagued her ever since she first cracked the drive from Lexsys.

"Have you had any sleep at all, Chi?" She turned as Kaiden walked up to her and offered her a plastic cup. She took it and inhaled the aroma of the coffee.

"I've had a couple of hours, but sleep was never much of a necessity for me," she responded and took a sip gratefully.

"You're supposed to hack into robots, not act like one," he quipped and sat on the bench beside her. "Unless method acting is a part of your training."

"It's a potential side effect of using the technician's suite too much, actually. It causes issues to the limbic system of the brain that helps control emotions."

He eyed her cautiously. "Seriously?"

"No, not really," she confessed and took another sip. "Although it can lead to a coma."

"Let's try to avoid that too," he suggested and closed the port window as the early morning sun began to rise. "So, you're all right with the current plan?"

"For how little of a plan it really is, yes." Chiyo put her cup down and leaned back. "I hope Indre won't be bothered that Operation Infiltration has become such a by the numbers mission."

"I think she's simply happy that it rhymes." Kaiden chuckled. "After all, I don't think anyone can get mad that the mission has a higher chance of all of us coming out unscathed. Unless something happens that botches the attack, of course."

She pointed to the hologram. "There is a possibility. We don't know what kind of force we'll have to deal with. Even after we make our way in, we'll have to fight our way out."

"That's not much of a deterrent, to me or anyone else." He glanced at the door that led to the bay. "Maybe to you and Indre because you prefer the cloak and hacker approach. But I hope it's too late to take it back."

Chiyo laughed. "Not much seems to shake you, Kaiden. What if there's a fleet of Goliath droids in there?"

He thought about it. "That might actually be helpful. It would make destroying the place a cinch."

"Some kind of invading alien force?"

"You realize we're traveling with aliens right now, don't

you?" he reminded her with a smirk. "That kind of thought lost its luster about eighty years ago."

"Fair enough." She stretched and turned the device off. "I want to thank you, Kaiden."

"You already have, even before we took off for Vox."

"I know that you've used your personal funds to help," she replied. "Not to mention doing Julio's little errand and any other promises to get the ship."

"He'll have to pay to fix my jacket," he grumbled. "But it's all good. I don't have a contract anymore, so the creds are mine to do with as I please. I have good gear and still have room and board until graduation, so helping a friend out seems like a good investment."

Chiyo smiled and looked at her tablet with the Nexus logo background "You already seem to know what you want to do. I'm curious, though. Why do you stay at the Academy?"

"I can still learn things and can always get better," he explained. "There's also the fact that it looks good to have it as something to brag about. It will help to bring in good gigs in the future. I need to actually graduate to be able to brag, though."

She nodded. "I see you do have some business sense."

"Besides, I've grown fond of all of you," he added, leaned his head back, and smiled. "Think of how bored you'd be if I wasn't around."

The infiltrator chuckled. "Among other things, I'm sure."

"I'd be happy to risk a horrible death for all of you, assuming I don't actually die a horrible death. I can only do that once." He grinned.

"Morning, friends," Genos announced over the comms. "We are approaching our destination. However, there doesn't appear to be a facility."

Kaiden and Chiyo looked at each other with concern. He immediately turned to the window and opened the blind. They looked at the landscape below.

"It's barren?" she whispered.

The area was a desolate, ravaged city with no noticeable life around. "It's a junk town," he confirmed.

"Did I have the wrong coordinates?" she wondered aloud.

"I doubt it, but let's go to the cockpit."

"Greetings friends," Genos said cheerfully as the duo entered. "I don't see anything that resembles the hologram friend Chiyo showed me. That is a pity. I very much looked forward to the potential destruction."

"Genos with a bloodlust. That's either very exciting or concerning," Kaiden quipped.

"I checked the signal again. It's definitely here." Chiyo looked out the window. "But I don't see anything that looks like it and nothing here seems to have active power of any kind."

"Underground," he responded and narrowed his eyes in an attempt to see better. "Or they are using some kind of device to cover their emissions somehow."

"Might I butt in?" Chief asked. *"I can't detect anything up here, but between me and the fox, we should be able to trace powerlines that might go through the ground."*

"*That is a good idea, madame,*" Kaitō added, speaking from Chiyo's tablet. "*Even if they are using a central core, once we get close enough, we would still be able to detect the general area even if they can hide it from scans.*"

The trio looked at each other. "I'll get suited up," the ace said. "Genos, try to land on the most stable structure available."

"By the looks of it that would be the street," the pilot replied.

"And please try to not scrape the ship. I'm already planning one risky mission. I'd rather not have the next one be returning the craft."

"I repaired as much as I could," Flynn said and handed Jaxon his chest plate. "Most of the repairs are replacement parts. I didn't have time to adjust the color."

"You did fine work, Flynn." The ace thanked him and placed it on the bench. "I didn't know you had skills in armorcraft."

"It's not my forte, but as an ace, you probably know that every class has to have a wide variety of skills to help them out in the field. And us marksman don't usually have the luxury of dropping our armor off in the middle of a mission."

"And I got my babies working again," Indre said enthusiastically and held her drones up. "Although oh-one makes a weird static noise."

"I'm sure it's fine," Kaiden assured her and holstered Debonair.

"It's begging for death," Chief stated.

"And it can have it once we're done here," he muttered in a low enough tone that the agent wouldn't hear.

"Damn humanist."

"So, this base is either hiding inside a barrier or is underground. That'll complicate things," Flynn commented.

"It simply means you won't be able to have a perch," the ace responded.

"Which means we won't have long-range support," Jaxon added.

"Which means you'll have to get out of your comfort zone," Indre teased.

Flynn waved her off. "You saw me both at the Ramses building and at the arena. That's not the handicap you think it is." To accentuate his point, he pressed a switch on his rifle and shortened the barrel.

"Just remember to raise hell," Kaiden ordered. "We're here to tear this place apart while Chiyo and Indre try to find any data they can. If nothing else, we'll leave a message of our own for these assholes."

"And be safe, all of you," Chiyo interjected and the group turned to her. "I don't like going in as blind as we are."

The ace smiled as he activated his rifle. "You told me you believe in your friends before we left right? You haven't changed your opinion, have you?"

Jaxon rubbed the back of his neck. "I did lose at the arena."

"That was supposed to be an inspiring moment, Jaxon." Kaiden groaned.

The infiltrator smiled and placed a hand on his shoulder. "I still do. That hasn't changed. But remember what you told me about who this might be. It could be bigger than we realize."

He took a moment to look at her before he gave a confident smirk. "That simply means we need to leave a bigger impression."

CHAPTER TWENTY-SIX

"*H*oly hell, there are a lot of power lines," Chief gasped as the team ventured deeper into the junk town.

"*Madame, I would hazard to guess that some of these simply lead to auxiliary stations or devices,*" Kaitō added. "*Only a few will possibly lead us to our destination.*"

"Is there any way to differentiate their paths and what they might be connected to?" Chiyo asked. Flynn paced behind her and his gaze searched constantly for possible snipers.

Chief's eye began to spin. "*I think I have one. Get on your knees, Kaiden.*"

"Could you word that differently?" his partner requested.

"*Hump the floor.*"

"Good God, I'll kneel. Please don't make it sound worse." He complied and focused on the artificial light of the lines through Chief's vision. "What are you doing? Can you see something special if you're clos— Whoa!" He raised his hand instantly to his head and almost doubled over.

"Kaiden! Are you all right?" Chiyo asked and knelt beside him to offer her support.

He took a deep breath and nodded. "Yeah, but it's…you know that feeling when you stand up too quickly? Imagine that but way worse."

"Sorry. I should have thought about feedback to you now," Chief apologized. *"I have a reading, though. It's fairly obvious, but see that fat one on the side there? That travels to a massive generator, one that needs to disperse energy constantly or it would implode on itself. That's gotta lead to our mystery facility."*

The ace stood and rubbed the back of his helmet—not that it made any difference, but the motion helped him think. "You can tell all that from a closer look?"

"It's the emission. Pumping that much energy will cause tiny amounts to pour out, even if it's properly insulated. Most devices wouldn't pick it up, but the implant is rather sensitive, considering its connection and all."

"I'm a living barometer now?"

"I think you'd be closer to a wattmeter," Indre informed him cheerily.

"It's weird either way," Flynn added.

"Even if we follow the line, I assume it'll be hidden once we reach a certain point," Jaxon pointed out.

"Certainly. But once we find that location, we can proceed from there. If it is hidden behind a barrier, we can find a way to access it. If it's underground…" Chiyo looked ahead, deeper into the town. "I'm sure there's an elevator or stairway that will lead us there in one of the buildings."

"Perhaps a teleporter?" Flynn suggested.

Indre shook her head. "That gives off a distinct reading so there's no way to hide that. It would defeat the point if they have gone out of their way to keep this place a secret."

"The line goes on for several more blocks. Keep your guard up," Chief warned.

The group looked at each other and nodded. Those who didn't already brandish their weapons drew them as they continued their search.

"It looks like the trail ends here." Kaiden surveyed the area. Six buildings sprawled around them with several behind those and a few more in the distance. "It looks like the line goes straight down. Whoever said underground lair wins the pool."

"So should we fan out and start looking?" Indre asked.

"I'll let you know if I find any suspicious bookcases," Flynn offered and began to walk to the buildings on the left.

"Hold on for a moment, friend Flynn," Genos called and removed a device from his belt.

The ace frowned at what looked like a metallic bug of some kind. "Uh, what is that?"

"It's a seeker. It targets devices between certain ampere that I set," he explained and pressed a button. The device floated up and then away.

"So it's a flying wattmeter," Indre quipped and looked at Kaiden. "It has you beat there."

"I didn't see it find the line we were looking for," he retorted and folded his arms.

"Correct. All that energy would have made the variables quite wide and confused the sensor. It would have simply flown around in circles." The mechanist followed the device, which headed toward the buildings on the right. The team fell in behind him. "But I assume that wherever they are hiding their entrance, there is some kind of terminal or switch that needs to be activated to access it, which uses much less power."

"That's nifty," Indre admitted. "I should consider getting one. I generally use power tracers."

"We engineers mainly use it to assist in construction and repairs. It just so happens that it is helpful in tracking in these kinds of desolate areas," the Tsuna explained. They entered the second building. The seeker flew to the back of the first floor and attached to a shattered picture in the back of the room. Genos walked up to it, removed the device and deactivated it, and set it to one side before he pulled on the picture. "It's bolted in."

"A cover?" Jaxon asked.

"A safe assumption, kin." He activated his gauntlet and extended the claw, gripped the side of the frame, and pulled. The picture came off and he tossed it on the floor. The team stared at a scanner now visible where the artwork had been.

"I wonder if every henchman has to rip that off to get in." Flynn chuckled.

"I assume they have a device that causes the portrait to move," the mechanist responded. He glanced around the room and dragged a finger along the wall, then examined the dust. "And I also assume it's been some time since anyone has come out, at least this way."

"How will we get in?" the marksman asked and peered at the scanner.

Kaiden held a thermal grenade up. "I have an option."

Indre pushed his hand down as she walked past him. "Save it for whatever is inside. I've got this." She stopped in front of the device and retrieved a circular pad which she held up to it. After a moment, the scanner illuminated, and a part of the wall slid up to reveal an elevator.

Kaiden stowed the grenade. "Well, that's certainly more subtle, at least."

"So this would be the point of no return, then?" Flynn inquired and took a moment to check his rifle once again.

"I'm almost certain they are at least aware of our presence," Jaxon pointed out and glanced at the ceiling. "If they haven't actually tracked us all along."

"We already agreed that this would get loud really quickly," Kaiden reminded him. "And I'm not climbing in vents this time."

"If they are tracking us already, we shouldn't waste time looking for another entrance," Chiyo stated and pointed at the elevator. "But we don't have to be obvious in our strategy either."

"Well. It looks like they finally made their way here." Dario sounded smug as he spun his chair away from the holo-screen. "Please feel free to have fun while you work."

"We—I underestimated them before." Yvette snorted and drew her blade. "I'll kill them quickly and be done with this."

"That is also a viable strategy," he conceded and picked a box up from the table. "But remember that this is a production facility. We have some bots and a few ghouls ready to go, but there isn't exactly much backup should you need it."

She opened the visor on her helm and glared at him. "You will keep the leader occupied, correct?"

"The plan is still the same," he assured her. "My guess is that Kaiden will run around with one or two of his friends, so the rest are yours. And should you eliminate them quickly, you might make it back in time to deal the killing blow. That would be a pleasant day for you, wouldn't it?"

The woman turned away and her visor snapped closed before she leapt up to the walkway above and to their left. "She's quite excited, in her own way," he noted as he strolled slowly toward the door. "I do hope she lives. I quite like her."

Once the elevator reached the bottom, a group of Havoc droids activated and fired at the doors to shred it with laser fire. As soon as they stopped and approached the wreck, two drones soared overhead and dropped thermals at their feet, which erupted quickly and destroyed the preliminary guards. The top of the elevator opened, and Indre and Flynn dropped out. He aimed immediately, ready to fire at any remaining droids, but was greeted by an empty chamber bathed in red light.

"Well. That's not much of a welcome," he quipped and lowered his weapon.

"This place could be mostly automated," Indre guessed as her drones returned to her. "It's hard to spill secrets if there aren't that many people who know the secret."

"If there are any, there'll be even less soon." Kaiden dropped from above with the others. "It should be fine, though. Their secrets will be safe with us."

CHAPTER TWENTY-SEVEN

Two dots moved left and four down the main hall. Yvette tucked the radar away and continued her pursuit, moving quickly, her footsteps silenced by the mods in her suit. She took out a small drone and directed it to fly off to pursue her quarry. While she had her orders and her targets, she wanted so badly to destroy Kaiden. The hatred she felt for him was one she couldn't really explain. All of them were responsible for their failure on the last mission. Of her teammates, two were dead and the others in jail.

Now, she worked as an underling for a man who treated her with supreme indifference. She was merely a tool for him, but she was used to that role. What angered her was that she couldn't do anything about it. He could kill her with a snap of his fingers, and she hated that she couldn't find the rage to even attempt to retaliate.

But what use would an attack be if she couldn't make a scratch before she died?

Perhaps in this situation, Kaiden could be a boon. If he

was able to eliminate Dario, she could not only free herself but use his tools to find Bastion. Once he was free, they could raise a new force together and annihilate these fanatics she had been trapped with for months.

Her drone found the targets. Two of them were definitely Tsuna as they had infusers. One was the agent, judging by the gadgets on her, and the last was clearly a marksman. That meant that Kaiden and Gendo's daughter were the ones who had separated from the group. She checked her map and confirmed that Dario was already moving to intercept them.

They could have this job done in ten minutes. She would not bide her time any longer. Dario would die or make good on his promise. Her patience was at its end.

"Do you have a destination or are we still winging it?" Kaiden asked as he brought his foot down hard on the head of a downed Soldier droid.

"We have a number of possible targets," Chiyo informed him and turned to check behind them. "The Genesis device is pinging a multitude of terminals, servers, nodes, and whatever you can dream of. This place seems to be run autonomously, which is unbelievable in a facility this vast."

"No kidding. There doesn't seem to be more than a couple of floors, but it's damn spacious." He peered at the ceiling more than fifty feet above him, illuminated in red light. "Do you think it was designed to be ominous?"

"The structure is built to be fortified against a potential cave in. Whoever designed it was quite thorough—and also coerced, if I had to guess." She glanced quickly at the device. "Kaiden, something just activated."

"Where?"

"Ahead—about thirty yards." She motioned down the long hall. "That door on the right."

He vented his rifle. "Do you think it's another batch of droids?"

"Perhaps, but this reading appears to be something more than only a power unit. It looks to be a mainframe."

"Well, I guess we'll start there." The duo made their way cautiously to the room and stood on either side of the doors. Chiyo nodded to him and sent Kaitō into the panel to gain access. As soon as the entrance opened, Kaiden twisted around the doorframe. The room was in darkness and Chief activated the night vision in his helm so he could check the area. "It looks like there's some kind of checkered pattern on the walls and there are a few terminals around." he lowered his gun as they entered. "I guess you can take a look at those and see if you can get anything from them because other than that, it's empty."

The doors behind them shut and locked as soon as they entered, and he whipped around. "I thought Kaitō had control?"

"*I do,*" the EI insisted. "*A command of higher authority must have come from an attached device or console.*"

The lines on the wall began to light up. Chiyo readied her sub-machine gun as the room changed and white constructs formed around them. One blocked their exit.

"What the hell are these?" the ace asked.

"Hard light constructs," she informed him. "In short,

holograms you can physically interact with but which can only take simple shapes. Usually, skins are—"

The constructs completed their formation before they began to glow. The room exploded in white light. Kaiden's helmet hastily deactivated the night vision. When the two opened their eyes, they stood in an alley and dark skies drizzled rain on them.

He held a hand up. The rain struck his palm but disappeared on impact. "Weird. Do you see this shit, Chi?"

Her attention was focused away from him and on a glowing blue neon sign behind them that emblazoned a kanji message. 未来.

"Mirai," she whispered. "That's the kanji for Mirai."

The ace surveyed their surroundings quickly. Someone was playing with them. At a flicker of movement down another path in the alley, he immediately aimed, ready to fire. A figure walked out clad in black medium armor, a set he recognized. "It's those ghouls again," he muttered and charged a blast. He located two above and another approaching from the left.

He prepared to fire, but Chiyo held a hand up. "Wait a moment," she said and raised the Genesis device. The golems above took aim, while the one Kaiden had in his sights raised its hand. A plasma blade activated from its gauntlet and the edges glowed red.

"Chi," he warned, redirected his rifle to cover the two above, and drew Debonair to aim at the one approaching them.

She pressed a button on the device and it beeped rapidly, then fell silent. The golems stiffened before the one in the alley collapsed. Those perched on the roof toppled soundlessly and landed with two consecutive thumps. The final adversary followed suit a second later.

Kaiden released the trigger slowly and his charged blast faded. "What did you do?"

"I learned that the signal I was able to get from the neurotech device helped to transmit commands to other receptor devices near it," she explained and grimaced at her potential assailant. "I assumed it was to direct these things and simply blocked it using a different wave."

"You are quite clever, aren't you?" They both froze when a voice spoke from above. "I had hoped I wouldn't have to get my hands dirty, but I admit that my excitement to take you on myself negated that somewhat."

The ace vaulted onto the top of a stack of crates, launched himself up, and grasped the edge of the roof on one of the buildings. He hauled himself up and scanned the area before his scrutiny settled on a man dressed in a dapper silver coat, white leggings, and a wide-brimmed silver hat. He couldn't make out his face from this distance, but he could see the wide, eerie smile as he returned the scrutiny.

"It's a pleasure to finally meet you in person, Kaiden," he announced with a bow and peered over to the ground. "And to you as well, *mio caro*. My name is Dario."

Kaiden aimed Sire at their new adversary. "Are you one of the guys after the Mirai Zaibatsu?"

"I was—still am, I suppose." The man straightened. "Right now, I am tasked with dealing with the intruders who are a threat to Earth's safety."

"Earth's safety?" he asked while he charged a shot.

"Well, that's what my boss and most of the others think.

I see their point but to be honest, I'm only here for my own pursuits," he admitted casually, folded his arms, and clasped both elbows. The man wore some kind of gauntlet on both hands. "I'm no humanitarian, really, although I like humans—or, at least, only certain ones. The rest bore me, for the most part. My boss is a good example. He's a splendid man. A real passion burns in him." He moved one hand to his lips. "And Gin Sonny, of course." He moved his hand from his lips in a dramatic gesture and made a kissing noise. "Magnifico! A pity he didn't live long enough for us to meet."

"You liked that crazy bastard?" he mocked. "Oh, well, there's no use trying to get information out of an insane person."

Dario smiled and his gauntlets flared with light.

"Kaiden, wait!" Chief shouted.

The ace released the trigger, his blast on a sure course toward Dario. It detonated only a few yards from the barrel, caught in a net of amber light and the eruption extinguished the light. His eyes widened as he was engulfed in the explosion and only dimly heard Chiyo call out to him.

CHAPTER TWENTY-EIGHT

"Is anything there, Indre?" Flynn called into the room.

"Only some random processing data. This one is another bust." She sighed.

"More are coming," Genos warned at the clank of droids approaching in the distance.

"We still have a little entertainment, then." The marksman chortled and readied his rifle. "There I was, all hyped up, but so far, this makes the arena feel like—"

"Flynn, look out!" Indre shouted and shoved him out of the way as drone oh-two swooped in and was cut in half in midair as a figure landed and rolled back. Drone oh-one prepared to fire, but a smaller mechanical collided with it and burrowed through before it targeted Genos. The mechanical was shot in flight by Jaxon and parts scattered around them.

Flynn and Indre stood and aimed at the assailant. The woman was dressed in a sleek black suit with a white line that traced from the top of the shoulders to the bottom of the legs. Her helmet was curved with a large visor on the front that slid away to reveal dark eyes glaring at them. "That would have been a quick kill, Agent. You robbed your friend of that."

Indre glared at her. Jaxon walked up and noticed the blade. "You're the assassin from Rasmus."

"The EX-10?" Flynn growled. "I thought we were done with those bastards."

Their adversary held her blade up and it began to glow blue.

"Friends, the droids," Genos shouted.

"Indre, help Genos deal with them, but be wary. Flynn, take her down," the ace ordered.

"With pleasure." The marksman fired three shots, but the assassin dodged them easily and closed in. Jaxon moved into her path and fired his machine gun. She spun aside and lunged forward to sink her blade into his ribs. The Tsuna drew his heavy pistol and blind-fired to his left. His opponent raised a hand to activate a small shield that blocked the blasts as she jumped back. Flynn took aim, but the barrier vanished, and she aimed at the sniper. A bolt fired from her gauntlet and struck across his rifle and into his shoulder. He hissed in pain but yanked it out as Jaxon forced the woman back with another volley from his machine gun.

"Are you all right?" he asked, his attention firmly on the assassin.

"It didn't get too deep. That's what the armor is for." He gritted his teeth as he examined the bolt. "It's barbed, though. That could have been really bad."

"Can you still—"

"Fight? Of course, mate." He checked his rifle and

cursed. "Hell, she severed the vents. It's too dangerous to fire using the energy core." He cracked the weapon open. "Give me a minute to switch out to kinetic—look out!"

The assassin disappeared—or rather her hologram did. When had he lost sight of her? Jaxon looked up as she plummeted toward him, her blade ready to pierce his eye. Her momentum was stopped when Geno's claw caught her in the air. The mechanist swung his cannon up and fired a blast, but she swung her arms, caught him by both sides of his helmet, and hurled him to the floor. She produced a blade from her other arm and plunged it into his chest.

Jaxon's eyes widened. *"Genos!"*

Kaiden's hearing was dulled but he heard gunfire. He forced himself up and stared in confusion as pieces of his helmet fell onto the fake ground. "What the hell happened?"

"An explosion. I was able to divert all the armor's energy into the shields, but they still didn't hold up," Chief explained. *"Get yourself together, partner, Chiyo is alone right now and this guy is fighting with nanos."*

"Nanos? What was that light?" He used the wall to prop himself up.

"The energy the nanos contain. He linked it together like a net to catch your shot and blow it up in your face. The nanos added to it. I should have seen it sooner, but they had no power until he activated them."

He dragged in a breath and took stock. His jacket was in tatters and his armor was now mostly compromised.

Debonair was still functional and his grenades seemed all right, luckily. They would have finished the job, without a doubt. "Do you see Sire?"

"Behind you, but it doesn't look like it'll be any help now."

"I needed to get an upgrade anyway. Wolfson will be pissed, though." He drew Debonair. "Where is he?"

"Still up top. Chiyo's chasing him around. She's prepping something but she can't focus on it right now."

"Then I'll buy her time. Maybe we should activate the Battle Suite."

"No can do, partner. You don't wanna go near those nanos with that—it's like giving them an open door."

The ace didn't understand that but now wasn't the time for explanations. Instead, he merely grimaced and forced himself to sprint but stopped when he noticed the motionless golems. He swiped both rifles from them and made his way to the roof.

"I must compliment you, Chiyo. You are quite nimble for someone of your class." Dario used some nanos to form a blaster and fired several shots at the infiltrator, who danced around them and fired in response. He moved his hand and scattered the nanos before he formed them into three spears that he launched toward her.

She jumped from the roof to the ground and was able to dodge two of them before she threw herself back to avoid the third. The spear barely scratched the surface of her visor before it drove into the ground. For a brief moment, the checkered pattern of the room's floor showed through before it was replaced by cracked rock once again. After a slow, deep breath, she pushed to her feet and checked the Genesis device. She still needed to calibrate it, but she couldn't find the time while he continued his assault.

"Tell me, Chiyo, did I get the atmosphere right?" Dario asked. He stood on the edge of the building and looked down at her. "I wanted to make it at least somewhat pleasant, but I'm working with an aesthetic I'm not really familiar with."

She reached casually behind her to activate the Genesis device. If he wanted to talk, she would use the time for set up. "Is this supposed to distract me?" she asked and triggered Kaitō to begin the process in the device. "You obviously based this on Tokyo, and I saw the sign with my father's company logo on it."

He looked around. "I paid a visit to a business district before leaving. That was the image I had in my head when I booted this holoroom up."

"You were in Tokyo?" she gasped and aimed her weapon at him. "Did you do anything to my father?"

"What? Of course not, *dolcezza*," he stated, his hand over his heart. "I actually didn't even have the chance to meet him before I had to rush over here to meet you. But I have to say I'm much happier with you, honestly. You're making this enjoyable."

"Madame, explosives!" Chiyo whirled and narrowed her eyes at several small orbs that hurtled toward her. She snatched a small spike from her belt and thrust it into the ground to release a forcefield and the orbs erupted on impact. The field shrank but held with each successive

blast. Who was this man? Someone who used nanos like this should use a device that was easy to hack into—an automated device that would enable her to take control of the nanos. But when she tried to hack into it, she saw that not only were his gauntlets well secured, but he only used pre-made designs and manual controls. He shouldn't be able to create and direct this many nanos at a time and definitely not so efficiently.

She flung herself out of the protective field before it broke and raced into another alley, torn between two conflicting priorities. While she had to get back up to the roof, she also needed to check on Kaiden. She hoped that she had diverted their assailant's attention away from him, but with how he was able to use his machines, he could have sought him out while she was focused on the battle.

Her thought was interrupted by a loud explosion but from the distance this time. For a moment, she feared the worst until a message popped up from Chief.

"Do what you need to. Let's get this bastard."

Kaiden tossed a thermal up and down in his hand. "You thought that was enough to kill me?" he roared and lobbed the thermal at Dario, who created another wall with his nanos to shield himself from the blast.

"I had hoped not, but I've had quite the fun time with your friend," the man responded. "You keep throwing those at me. I assume your EI has told you about my nanos?"

Chief had certainly done so, but with the vision the EI

granted him, he could also see them—thousands of tiny lights filled the sky.

"I imagine you think you can whittle them down. A fine idea, I suppose. I do have a finite amount," he confessed and created several explosive orbs as he spoke. "But can you do it quickly?"

He arced the orbs toward the ace, who raised the rifle he'd taken from the golem. The missiles flew in erratic patterns in an attempt to confuse him, but he annihilated them with ease before he lobbed his last thermal at Dario. The assailant smiled as he formed another wall to defend himself. When the blast erupted, he dismissed the shield and created more spears but Kaiden threw the rifle itself at him. It glowed red and the man snickered as he quickly remade his shield. He let the overloading rifle explode before he opened the shield to discover that his quarry had gone.

Without warning, he was struck from the side by several blasts that seared through his armored jacket. He moved his nanos to block the rest of the shots, but pain already burned in his side. His smile, however, didn't falter. He straightened and ignored the blood that ran down his chest and leg as he searched for his opponent.

The ace stood on the opposite rooftop with another rifle and vented it as he raised Debonair. "Will you take this seriously now?"

Dario looked at him. Up until this point, he had merely been the target of a mission. Now, he stood as a worthy opponent. He studied the young soldier with glee on his face. "*Magnifico*."

CHAPTER TWENTY-NINE

"This weak piece of junk." Kaiden hissed his annoyance and vented the rifle he'd appropriated. "They thought this would be enough to kill us?"

"You severely underestimate the power of that weapon, Kaiden," Dario responded as he jumped from his perch. His nanos swirled around him. "That or you underestimate the effectiveness of my fashion." He laughed and traced the folds of his jacket.

"Are you simply taking comfort in the knowledge that you'll die pretty?" The ace aimed the rifle once more and snapped the vent shut. "I don't exactly know how you control those things. The gauntlets obviously play a part, but you aren't moving that quickly, which makes you an easy target once I have that figured out."

"It takes a fair amount of concentration since I don't control them by traditional means. You're quite right on that, *mio amico,*" the man confessed and twirled a hand in the air as if he tried to pet the multitude of miniscule machines around him.

"Chief, I thought translations were on," Kaiden murmured.

"He's speaking English for the most part. I think he simply adds the Italian for flavor or something."

The ace sighed. "As long as his last words are 'dammit, I'm dying,' I don't really care what language it's in."

"Tell me, Kaiden," Dario began and spread his arms wide. "Have you ever faced an opponent like me?"

"Overconfident jackasses? Yeah, most of them are," he replied and released the trigger. The blasts struck a shield of amber energy in front of his opponent.

"I referred to my weapon of choice," the man retorted. "I started this fight with one hundred thousand nanos. I'm now down to about forty-seven thousand." He glanced at Kaiden's waist. "You seem to be out of grenades, so I'll ask again. Do you believe you can whittle down the rest with only laser fire?"

Kaiden's hope was that Chiyo would be able to find a way around them. He needed to make contact with her, but he had received no reply yet. For now, the best he could do was continue to stall. He fired several more shots and all of them were simply blocked by the shield.

"I should let you know that I can create fields by expanding the energy inside them to one another," his adversary revealed and clicked his fingers as several blasters formed above him, all aimed at the ace. "Although you seem quite intelligent. I'm sure you're already aware of that."

"Why do the guys with the fancy weapons always insist on bragging about them?" he grumbled and vented the rifle as he looked for escape options. "I probably could have, but Chief filled me in plenty."

"Ah, yes, your EI." Dario almost purred the words as the blasters above him began to charge. "My boss was quite interested in that."

"What for?" he demanded. "Are you one of those Arbiter guys Laurie was talking about?"

"Kaiden, you need to retreat," Chief warned.

"What for? We need to buy Chiyo time."

"Pay attention. Some of the nanos have broken off and are floating your way." He peered at small clusters of light that hovered slowly around him.

"They aren't that powerful by themselves, right? That's why he keeps making stuff with them."

"He's trying to get them inside you, through orifices or wounds," the EI explained. *"They can't move that quickly on their own. But if he gets enough into you, he can simply detonate them and kill you from the inside. That's why I said not to use the Battle Suite. The heightened condition gives them much easier access because they're drawn by the energy."*

Kaiden glanced around hastily and decided he had a few spare seconds. He reached to the back of his belt. "Chief, can shocks do anything to these nanos?"

"They will disable them temporarily. I'm sure he'll have the ones that are still working reactivate them."

"That'll do." He retrieved one of the two static mines he'd borrowed from Indre's stash, flung it at the shield, and fired at it to cause it to erupt. The shield protecting Dario shut down and the ace leapt off the edge of the roof, drew Debonair, and fired four quick shots before he fell out of view. He flipped, landed smoothly, and raced down the alley to a central plaza.

A rapid volley behind him confirmed a further attack. He closed the vent of his rifle and rolled out of the way. One of the shots caught the top of his foot and melted away the little remaining armor. He turned and fired at the pursuing blasters and managed to destroy half of the six. The other three spread out and continued the onslaught. A standing billboard would provide some cover, he realized, whether the machines were automated or not. He sprinted toward it while he maintained a steady stream of fire behind him One of his shots struck home, but the scorched nanos simply fell while the rest reformed into a smaller blaster. The mechanicals were persistent even in the face of determined retaliation.

Kaiden made it into the cover of the billboard but the shots penetrated it easily, which wasn't surprising, but it did serve his primary purpose, which was merely to get out of clear view. He vented his rifle—prematurely as he still had a few shots left, but if he had another opportunity to take a shot at Dario, he didn't want to risk being over-heated. A whistling sound alerted him, and he ducked as two spears tore through the billboard. They immediately disassembled and transformed into bombs.

"Shit!" he cursed and flung himself away as they exploded. He escaped direct injury, but the force hurled him farther down the plaza. With no time to catch his breath, he rolled, slammed the vent shut, and fired at the blasters before they could attack and obliterated them. He grimaced at a field of lights above him that almost covered the sky.

"This is the worst." He grunted morosely and pushed to his feet to prepare for an attack.

"He might not be very mobile, but if he keeps his opponents at bay, that doesn't seem to be a problem," Chief commented.

"It makes it my problem, though," he muttered. "Any word from Chi?"

"I just got one from Kaitō. He says she's almost ready but there's nothing she can make quickly that will stop them permanently. She'll release a signal that will pause them temporarily."

"They'll only freeze, then?"

"For a minute, maybe."

He nodded and remained focused on the hovering nanos. "That'll be enough. Tell her to let me know when she's ready and I'll tell her when to activate it."

Finally, a dozen of explosives formed above. The ace selected the remaining mine. "Hopefully, she's ready soon." He threw it as the bombs descended and fired at it seconds before the bombs erupted to release a wave of electricity that surged through the sky.

"Genos," Indre shouted, temporarily distracted from the droids. She turned quickly and fired one of her EMP missiles into the horde to deactivate several at once as she continued to fire to keep them away from her and the team.

Jaxon roared with frustration as he tried to fire his machine gun, only for it to fail from overheating. He threw it to the side, snatched up Genos' cannon, and fired at the assassin. The orb-shaped projectiles were easy for her to avoid and she even used her shield to redirect one of them at Flynn, who had prepared to fire. He evaded it with a jump but tumbled from the force when the blast struck the wall.

Yvette drew a pistol and aimed at the distracted Indre. Jaxon prepared to fire but hesitated for a moment, worried she would deflect it again and harm his teammates. He flicked his free hand and his blade slid from its compartment. In a swift, smooth motion, he reversed it in his palm, leaned back, and pitched it at their adversary as he yelled for Indre to move away.

Yvette caught the blade in her free hand as she fired with the other. Indre dove to the floor and the blast sailed over her and struck one of the remaining droids. The agent activated a shield device and held it above her as the assassin and six remaining droids released another round of shots. Jaxon swung the cannon to the droids, charged a shot, and fired at the floor. The blast destroyed four in a surge of energy and the other two were knocked back. Two well-placed shots through the head annihilated them. Flynn had recovered and gave him a thumbs-up.

Indre deactivated the shielding device as she rolled into a seated position and flung it at the assassin, who simply craned her neck to the side to dodge the makeshift projectile. Before the device reactivated, a blow from behind her thrust her forward. She planted one hand on the floor, flipped herself to the side, and retrieved her sword. The weapon swung as she whirled toward the remaining Tsuna in an attempt to cut him down. She cursed when her blade was caught and tried to yank it free from Genos, who grasped it firmly in his claw.

"It is rather fortunate that you don't seem familiar with my anatomy," he muttered and crushed the metal before he swiped at her. She ducked under the attack and fired two bolts from her gauntlet at Jaxon. They struck home, but if he was surprised or in pain, he didn't show it. Instead, he tossed his teammate his cannon as he drew his hand cannon. Yvette responded with a shot from her pistol aimed at the ace's helmet, which broke the shielding. She prepared to fire another when the pistol burst apart. Shards embedded into her hand through her suit. She glanced up with another loud curse as Flynn readied to fire another shot. Her HUD began to shimmer, and her visuals cut off before a burning pain flared in her back and she collapsed.

Indre stood and shook her arm as static surged across it. "Remind me to configure this gauntlet properly next time. The sucker delivers way too much output."

CHAPTER THIRTY

"Kaitō, tell him it's ready," Chiyo ordered as she raced down the alley. She winced at another explosion. "He had better not be dead."

"*At once, madame,*" the EI confirmed. "*You'll have to get quite close, yes?*"

"For it to be effective, yes. If I'm more than ten yards away from him, it'll only last seconds instead of a minute." As the alley narrowed, she vaulted onto a wall and quickly launched herself off to grasp the edge of a roof. She hauled herself up but was greeted by a blaster aimed directly at her and let go as it fired. Thankfully, she managed to land without injury.

"*Mio caro,* I wondered where you went," Dario called. The infiltrator armed herself with her sub-machine gun before she leapt onto the wall once again. This time, she jumped onto the next one and used that to launch herself to the opposite, taller building. She turned and fired at the blaster and the two new ones that had joined it and eliminated them as she landed. In a half-crouch she took a moment to survey the situation. He stood with his arms folded and smiled at her from approximately forty yards away.

At first, she felt a chill when she didn't see Kaiden, but after another explosion, he lunged from the smoke and landed only a couple buildings away from their adversary. He looked ready to fire on their attacker.

Are you ready? The message popped up on her visor and she looked quickly at her partner. He was focused on her and waited for a response. She nodded and held the Genesis device behind her back. The ace fired a concerted volley as she sprinted across the rooftops. The other man formed a shield to deal with the attack and created blasters and spears to pursue her at the same time.

Chiyo took out a static grenade and lobbed it behind her but was only able to demolish a couple of spears in midflight. The more agile blasters simply moved out of the way. Kaiden's rifle began to overheat. He opened the vent and drew Debonair to continue the attack and managed to shatter the shield, which was simply replaced by another.

"Kaiden, behind you." He looked back as a swarm of nanos closed in, no doubt sent to crawl their way into him. With a grimace, he lowered Debonair, walked up to the shield, and began beating on it to catch Dario's attention.

His opponent laughed merrily. "You really are tenacious, aren't you, Kaiden?" He raised an arm and a larger bomb began to form overhead. "You whittled it down to twenty-four thousand. That's quite an accomplishment. I might have had a little too much fun. Most of my work is in assassination, so I don't really get the chance to enjoy my—"

"Kaiden!" Chiyo shouted and both men looked at her as she raised the device.

"Do it!"

Dario glared at the infiltrator. "You shouldn't interrupt a good time." He growled his annoyance and sent a line of nanos toward her. They wound around her, immobilized her, and drew her closer to him. He studied her with a smug smile. "Are you jealous that I haven't given you your due?" he asked and his eyes glowed yellow. "You played your part well, but there's a bigger part waiting for you. I'll thank you properly once it's done."

"I should thank you," she retorted and pressed the switch on the Genesis device. "This was closer than I actually hoped to get." She sucked in her breath and forced herself out of the nanos' grip. They broke apart easily and Dario's eyes widened as he tried to summon more with no result.

He glanced at Kaiden who grinned at him, his rifle and Debonair in either hand, and began to fire. The assassin drew his jacket in close and lowered his head. The hail of lasers pummeled him relentlessly. For a moment, he seemed able to withstand it but was eventually hurled off his feet as his jacket began to shatter in a flurry of sparks.

The weapons overheated and the ace dropped the rifle and vented Debonair. Chiyo walked beside him with her sub-machine gun at the ready. Dario pushed onto his knees. He drew ragged breaths and blood poured from his chest and mouth. Despite this, he looked up with a smile. While obviously weary and haggard, it hadn't left.

"I'm beginning to see that I may have over-indulged," he said, his voice weak and labored. He looked at them as Kaiden placed Debonair's barrel against his forehead. "That was a wonderful dance, you two."

"You didn't answer my question." He shut the vent on Debonair. "Are you with the Arbiter Organization?"

Chiyo glanced questioningly at him, but Dario merely chuckled in reply. "A basic tenet of an assassin's code is to not give up their employer, no matter who they might be."

"That tells me enough. Although I would guess you did that deliberately. You have a weird code."

"I'm merely hoping we see each other again," the man said, and his smile widened. "It's been a while since I had a battle where I had to actually try."

"You should have tried harder." Kaiden sneered and pressed the barrel harder into his head. "You can live a little longer if you tell us why you were after those companies and what you have planned for Mirai."

"That sounds like such a boring way to spend an evening," Dario observed calmly. He licked his lips and smeared the blood. "Parties like this should have a grand finale, no?"

A bright flash left the duo momentarily disoriented and they stared around them in confusion. They were back in the checkered room. The ace spun and fired, but their adversary fell back as a small stream of nanos emerged from inside his jacket and formed into a bomb. Chiyo grabbed her partner and jumped back as it exploded. They bounced for a few yards before he found his footing and braced himself to catch her.

Red lights flashed above them and sirens blared. Something dropped with a distinctive clunk and a detonator rolled toward him. He glanced up as a smiling Dario waved at him from an exit on the other side of the room before the door began to shut. He fired but the man simply walked away, and the shots were blocked by the door and wall. With a muttered curse, he forced himself up to pursue, but his legs gave way as he felt a pain blaze in his chest.

"Kaiden, it's a detonation sequence. The core will overload," Chiyo warned him as she helped him up. "We have to go."

He lowered his gun, his limbs trembling. "I know, dammit. I know." She placed one of his arms around her shoulders and half-dragged him to the door they had entered through.

"Kaiden, Chiyo, are you there?"

"We're here, Jaxon," the infiltrator answered. "Where are you?"

"In the main hall. We ran into an assassin, but she's being dealt with," he replied.

Flynn looked at the assassin, who was now bound in a net provided by Indre. "Are you sure that'll hold her?"

"She is unarmed," Genos reminded him and held a drive up. "She had this on her. According to my EI, it contains considerable information."

"It seems foolish that they would let their members carry something like that around," Indre commented.

"I intended to take care of these madmen myself," Yvette responded, her gaze focused downward.

"She's conscious already?" Flynn asked. "Tough, isn't she?"

The agent knelt beside her. "Why would you want to take down your own employers?"

"I'm not here by choice or for the credits. I was made an offer and I am expendable," she muttered. "Once I had the opportunity, I intended to deal with them—to bring an army. Bastion had the connections."

"You can still be of use," Genos suggested and crouched next to Indre. "If those who extorted you are such frightening beings, what you know could be invaluable."

She looked at them and although she tried to maintain a stoic façade, the Tsuna noted fear. "I won't have the chance to say any—" Her eyes bulged. Indre reacted instinctively and shoved herself and Genos aside as Yvette threw her head back. An explosion destroyed the top of her helmet and blood oozed out like a trickling waterfall from the cracked remains of the headgear before the body toppled.

Dario sighed as he put the tablet away and made his way to the hangar. It really was most unfortunate that his charms weren't enough. He would simply have to make do with the golems now. The warning lights were all that illuminated the hall and he moved from a bright red to darkness. Blood dripped as he continued to walk, and his smile faltered for a moment. Merrick would probably be rather annoyed at this turn of events. He might lose a little of the trust he had in him and there would certainly be no cele-bratory drinks with nothing to celebrate.

His smile returned faintly. Perhaps Merrick wouldn't have anything to celebrate. But as he looked at the wounds he had sustained and felt the adrenaline that still pumped through him, he knew he certainly did.

CHAPTER THIRTY-ONE

"Chiyo, are you close?" Jaxon asked once he and his group had returned to the starting point.

"Quite close." The response didn't come from the comms but from his left. Kaiden was currently down to virtually only his underlay and held up by the infiltrator, who was also missing most of her armor.

"Friends, what happened to you?" Genos asked, concerned as he rushed over to help Chiyo support her partner.

The ace noticed the blood and stab wound in the mechanist's chest. "I could ask the same, Genos." He chuckled and pointed to the wound. "Are you all right?"

"Hmm? Oh, yes. I've treated it with rejuv serum until I can have it attended to properly," the Tsuna assured him. "Unfortunately, we were unable to secure much data. We were interrupted by an assassin before the alarms sounded."

"Yeah, that's my fault," he admitted.

Flynn sighed and slouched a little as he studied Kaiden. "Aw, come on, mate. What did you do this time?"

"I didn't shoot someone fast enough." He grunted. "Do we have a way out of here? I don't think the elevator is an option."

"Maybe not the traditional way," Indre stated and brandished a hook. "I'll climb up there and open the entrance. I have a Zeppelin I'll send down that will carry you up."

"I don't think we have much time," Genos remarked with a hasty survey of their surroundings. "Most detonation sequences are meant to purge a facility. It may take time to condense the energy, but once the explosion happens, it is extremely powerful."

"Then I recommend you have the ship ready," the agent countered and hooked herself to one of the cables in the shaft. "I'll be done in no time." She shinnied up the cable to the top.

"You know, she's amazingly calm considering the imminent death happening around us," Flynn noted.

"I think we all understand that panicking wouldn't be helpful right now," Jaxon replied.

"I'm desensitized, really," Kaiden admitted. "I've faced death about four times so far this year and a couple of times last year. I'm getting used to it."

"It might be a side effect of the realism of the Animus," Genos suggested as he held his tablet with his free hand and proceeded to boot the ship up. "We have all gotten used to violence."

"Still, I'd rather not go out like this. Amber would find a way to bring me back simply to kill me again." The marksman approached the elevator doors, stuck his head in, and looked up. "Hey, Indre, are you done yet?"

"Yeah, it's open. Chill for a second, would you? I'm sending the Zeppelin down."

Flynn stepped back as a floating orb with a handle on the bottom lowered within reach. He motioned Kaiden over. "You first, Kai. You're the most injured one here, which means you'll be the slowest."

"I'm fine," the ace protested and tried to straighten before Jaxon stepped up and poked a finger into his ribs. "Ow! What are you—"

"That was enough to harm you?" the Tsuna asked and studied him. The knowing scrutiny made him look away sheepishly. "Please get on the Zeppelin. It's one at a time and you're holding up the rest."

Kaiden sighed, nodded, and limped over to the device. "See you all up top," he promised with a wave as the Zeppelin pulled him up.

Chiyo watched him go, a little tense with worry. Genos moved closer and held out a closed hand. "Friend Chiyo, I'm not sure what you were able to find, but we got this from the assassin." He opened the hand to reveal a drive, which she took. "The assassin said she herself planned to target the group at some point, but she was killed remotely a few minutes after we defeated her."

She nodded and stowed the drive in her remaining compartment. "Thank you, Genos. Hopefully, this means we can finally track down whoever did this."

"Were you able to find any leads?" he asked.

She thought of what her partner had asked Dario about the Arbiter Organization. The only time she had heard the name was as a rumor of a shadowy cabal, one that most thought of as fiction or a long-dormant organization. "I may have something," she said tentatively. "But I need to see what's on here and ask some questions first."

"Do you think we can make it out in time, Genos?" Kaiden asked from the co-pilot's seat. "To miss the rubble and stuff. There's no use surviving if Julio will kill me anyway."

"I'm sure we will make it out of the immediate area in time," the Tsuna assured him as he finished checking the controls. "If any debris reaches us, I will make sure to avoid it."

"Thanks, Gee." He sighed, leaned back, and regarded his friend with new respect. "You know, even with the serum, you're taking that wound like a champ."

"I believe she aimed for our equivalent of the heart," he replied and eased the ship up. "Fortunately, it's not in the identical place as that of humans. It's more centered for us. Still, it hurts quite badly, I must say."

"Do you want me to take over?"

"You seem to be in worse shape, friend Kaiden," the mechanist noted, banked the ship toward the sky, and began the exit flight.

"That's a fair point." He sighed and tucked his arms closer together to apply pressure.

"Also, I believe I could lose an entire arm and still be a better pilot than you," Genos stated cheerfully.

Kaiden scowled. "Flynn has taught you bad things."

"It's merely an observation," the Tsuna responded as he

pulled the booster switch down and launched the ship upward. "If you would like to observe the explosion, you can look at this monitor—"

"Kaiden?" Chiyo walked into the cockpit and he turned to look at her. "Can I talk to you for a moment?"

"Sure, what do you need?"

She glanced Genos. "I hoped we could be alone."

The pilot nodded. "Oh, certainly, friend Chiyo. I can activate the autopilot and—" He stopped when the ace clapped a hand on his shoulder.

"I think she's asking me to go with her, but I appreciate it." He stood and followed her out of the cockpit and past the other team members in the bay, all of whom now took their armor off and checked their weapons. The vessel shuddered when the facility erupted beneath them. Kaiden caught himself against a wall and waited to hear any odd noises or bumps. He sighed with relief when none came. The duo entered the spare room and he sagged onto the bench. "What's up, Chi?"

She showed him the drive. "Genos said they recovered this from their attacker. I took a quick look and it has considerable material on her previous employers."

"The guys who ran that place? That's great," Kaiden responded enthusiastically. "That means we can dig something up to help your dad, right? I was worried this might have all been a bust."

"Kaiden, what is the Arbiter Organization?" she asked bluntly.

He looked at her and scratched his head, a little nonplussed by the forthright question. "All that stuff? It's something Laurie told me about. They might be the guys after me."

"After you?"

"I'm not sure if I'm top priority anymore but... You know what? It's a long ride so I might as well tell you everything."

She sat opposite him and he took a deep breath before he began the explanation. He told her about the glitches in the Animus during his first year, including the Asiton that attacked them during the Death Match, which were possibly all orchestrated by the AO to investigate him and the Animus. How Gin was probably brought in by them, in the first place, and that they were potentially the ones trying to take Mirai over and working on the golems.

Chiyo was silent through it all, almost motionless as she took in all the details. When he was finished, she simply sat and stared at the drive. "This has become...much larger than I could have imagined."

"And we didn't think it would be an easy thing at all," he agreed. "I didn't bring it up because it's all still only guesswork. Laurie and Sasha both seem to believe they are real, but whether they're simply a group using the name or the actual organization that's been dormant all this time, they couldn't say."

"Will you go after them?" she asked and caught him off guard.

"What? I mean... Not right now, if that's what you're—"

"No, I mean at all." She turned to face him. "Will you go after this organization if that's who this is?"

"Chi, whether it is or isn't them, they have to be

stopped," Kaiden stated. "We still have to find a way to do that."

"We've bought time by destroying that facility," she pointed out. "I'm sure that officials will come to investigate what happened due to the explosion. Even if they have more, I'm sure that's stalled their production of those golems. As for my father…" She looked at the device again. "I'm sure there's something on here I can send to him. With his connections, he will have no problem preparing for them for the time being. We've accomplished what I wanted to do, Kaiden. I'm worried about what you want to do."

"Worried? Chi, I'm reckless, not suicidal," he chided. "I don't even know where their main base is or anything like…" He trailed off and his attention drifted to the device. "It's on there, isn't it?"

"I'm not sure, but there are several locations mapped on here," she confirmed. "But I don't want you to go after them. You can't." Her words grew quieter as she looked down and clutched the drive harder.

"You'll break it," he warned and placed his hand over hers. "Chiyo, even if I didn't want to go after them, it's very clear that they are all about me and really want Chief for whatever reason."

"Could you get rid of—" She didn't finish her sentence, but Kaiden could understand. He didn't feel anger at the suggestion or even think it was ludicrous. He looked at her and recognized the very evident fear and concern. Something had really shaken her.

"Chi, look at me." She looked up and he held her gaze. "Go ahead and show her, Chief."

His HUD activated and she examined it for a moment. "They aren't EI contacts like yours. That's Chief himself," he explained, and her eyes widened. "After Gin's attack on the Animus, Chief had to do…something that basically fused him to my mind. Without him, I'm essentially braindead."

Chiyo gasped. "How is that even possible?"

"Chief can give you the rundown of the techno-jargon. But Laurie himself isn't completely sure," the ace admitted. "I would have had a hard time getting rid of Chief before now. As it stands, it is essentially impossible."

She looked away again and chuckled wryly. "You've had to keep a lot of secrets, haven't you?"

"I actually didn't know about it until the day you asked me to help you with this," he revealed. "I'm still trying to wrap my head around it myself. But I wanted you to know about it so you will understand when I say I can't simply try to forget about these guys. They seem to have big plans and as a merc, I'll probably have to clean up after them anyway." He placed a hand on her shoulder. "And like I said, they are after me and the Academy for whatever reason. I can't simply turn away. I'm not trying to be a hero or anything like that. Hell, I would even say it's for completely selfish reasons. I already lost a place I called home and lost people I cared about. I won't let that happen again."

"I suppose I can relate," she conceded and tried to smile when she looked at him again. "I also feel like I lost a place I called home. But the only person I cared about whom I lost was my mother—before I could really get to know her—and I have so few memories." She turned her closed fist, opened it, and took his hand that rested above it. "I'm scared of losing you."

Kaiden looked at their entwined hands for a moment, then offered her a smile. "Not to make light of this, but we all are in the industry of death and destruction."

For a moment, he worried when her smile dropped, but she began to laugh. "I suppose so. But I worry that if you should ever fall, I won't be there to help."

"I doubt I'd get the chance," he responded, leaned back against the wall, and drew her closer. "I'm actually tired of the secrets and all that. I'll go after them, Chi. I don't know when, exactly, but I won't wait around for them to come to me. That didn't turn out so well last time."

"I understand." Chiyo sighed and rested her head on his shoulder. "I need to stop them too."

He blinked for a moment before he laughed out loud. "Was all this simply a roundabout way to ask me to take you with me?"

"I suppose so," she confessed and grinned at him. "Will you?"

"Obviously, I always need a good hacker on the team," he replied. "And…well, I fight harder with you around."

"Same here," she said. After a moment, she turned and took out the Genesis device. "Do you want to see what's on here?"

He nodded. "Go ahead."

She placed the drive into the device and a holoscreen activated to display dozens of folders. All were cryptically marked, but she instantly opened one that revealed a map. Excitement shivered through him when dots appeared. "Oh, yeah. We can certainly use this."

CHAPTER THIRTY-TWO

"Sir, I brought them," Rei informed him and walked into the room with four men dressed in white coats. "These are the best and brightest in the cyber detective sector. They will have no problem finding out who—"

"I already know who has targeted us, Rei," Gendo responded and continued to read the document on his screen.

"Really, sir? You found out who the culprits are?" she asked.

"There is a facility here in Tokyo—twenty-two miles from this building in fact." He gestured to send the document to Rei and the detectives. "They are the ones who are responsible."

"Where did you find this, sir?" one of the detectives asked.

"I didn't. My daughter did." He stood from his desk.

"Chiyo?" Rei asked, shocked.

"We'll investigate this right away. Let's go," the leader of the group ordered, and they filed quickly out of the room.

Gendo walked to his favorite spot and looked out at the cityscape below. "It's quite unbelievable isn't it?"

Rei moved closer to the document and studied it carefully. "Chiyo was always a gifted hacker, but to find this is—"

"She is still looking out for us," Gendo whispered. "After everything."

"Sorry, sir?"

He turned to her. "It's nothing, Rei. Keep the security increased until this has been resolved. This is to be only a temporary fix for now."

"Understood. I'll let the others know," she said with a bow and turned to depart.

He held a hand out. "One more thing, Rei."

"Yes, sir?"

"I want you to make a donation to that Academy and send a message along with it."

Dario removed one of his nano arms, looked at the socket on it, and recalled briefly how he'd lost it. He glanced at the other arm, already replaced by his normal artificial limb. He had lost them both in one battle and almost died that day. It had been one of the few times he really had to outthink and maneuver an opponent. During his fight with Kaiden and Chiyo today, he could hear his own heart beating so rapidly and so rhythmically that he could almost dance to it. It was sublime.

"Sir, the leader is calling."

He attached the other arm, turned, and activated the pad on the table. Merrick appeared onscreen.

"I assume it didn't go as you imagined?" the man asked. If he was angry, he did a good job of masking it as always.

"Honestly, not at all," he admitted and leaned back in his chair with a smile. "But I haven't had that much fun in such a long time. I wonder if all the Nexus students are like that."

"Did you hold back, Dario?" his superior asked. "You did the right thing to destroy the facility if it came to that, but if it could have been avoided—"

"I played too much, I'll admit to that." He nodded and took a panatela cigar from a small golden box beside the pad. "Will you finally pull the trigger on the bomb in this ship?"

Merrick raised an eyebrow before he lowered his head and smirked. "So you discovered it, then?"

"The day you gave me this ship," he confirmed and cut into the tip with a deft motion. "I thought it would be rude to remove it."

"Always the gentleman," the other man muttered. He sighed and shook his head. "I disassembled the trigger a long time ago, but I regret it somewhat now that we've lost two facilities."

"Two?" Dario asked and lit the cigar.

"The one we had near Mirai has been compromised. Police are closing in as we speak," he explained. "I assume they were able to access and remove the data?"

"I didn't realize we had data on other facilities stored there," Dario stated calmly and exhaled a trail of smoke. "I was occupied with Kaiden and Chiyo. Yvette was responsible for the others."

"And where is she now?" his boss asked.

"Not with us, unfortunately."

"I see." Merrick closed his eyes and took a few deep breaths. "We have many accomplishments and victories and we've already made up for the few losses. But Kaiden has disrupted two important operations now. We'll need to deal with him, that EI be damned."

"Wow, you must be quite angry," he commented and twirled the cigar in his hand.

The leader rested his chin on his hand. "I was able to find breaches in some of the systems before the meltdown. But there shouldn't have been any information that was helpful to them in those devices."

"Perhaps they realized that they could have been monitored and their activities reported and so used different methods. The whole facility was automated, after all," he pointed out.

"Possibly. We'll need to make the proper changes to combat this in the future. I doubt we'll be able to work as effectively from the shadows from now on."

"Are you growing paranoid now, sir?" he teased.

"I'm always cautious, Dario." Merrick gave him a stern look. "When you return, get healed up and ready to move as soon as you can."

"I can go right now if you wish," Dario offered and took another puff.

"Have you ever heard the phrase 'the spirit is willing, but the flesh is weak?'"

He snickered. "In very specific circumstances, yes."

"You need to recover before I send you off again. Eagerness means nothing when strength cannot back it up."

"There you go again with those fancy words," he countered. "I'll return soon and be ready by tomorrow night."

"Understood. I look forward to it, Dario." Merrick stated crisply and signed off.

Dario stuck the cigar in his mouth and leaned back. They were already making use of the drive Yvette had stored data on. That was quick. Hopefully, Kaiden would find his way to him soon or would become enough of a bother that he was sent after him again. He wanted another dance.

"Thank you, Professor," Chiyo said with a bow as she handed the Genesis device back to him.

"My, this thing is banged up," Laurie commented cheerfully. "I'll have to reinforce the internals and make a harder shell."

"My apologies. This mission became much more chaotic than I thought it would," she stated and stiffened.

He cast a bemused grin at Kaiden. "Considering your company, I'm surprised it returned intact."

"Cute, Prof," the ace muttered and took a sip of the wine he'd been given. "Not bad."

The professor looked back at Chiyo, his eyes narrowed. "Were you able to find what you needed?"

"I was able to find some information on the group that had targeted my father's company—or developing the golems, at least," she explained as she retrieved the drive they'd recovered from the assassin and handed it to him.

"Another drive?" he asked and examined it casually. "At least this one looks normal."

"I think you'll like what's on it," Kaiden stated. "It proves you're not a crazy person. At least with your AO theory."

Laurie almost fell out of his chair with excitement. He immediately plugged the device into his console. "This has information on the organization?"

"Bits and pieces," Chiyo clarified. "It's only mentioned in a few places. This was recovered from an assassin who worked briefly for them. She said the group referred to themselves as the Arbiter Organization."

"Aurora, go through everything," Laurie commanded.

"At once, sir."

The professor reached for his pad. "I need to contact Sasha immediately."

"I heard, Professor." The commander spoke from behind them and Kaiden almost spilled his wine in surprise.

"How do you move that quietly?" he asked and set the glass carefully on the desk.

"Hard work," he replied and turned to Chiyo. "So, both of the free students are here."

"Free students?" Kaiden asked.

"As in you have no contract," Sasha stated. He strode behind Laurie's desk and peered at the monitor.

"No contract? I'm still contracted, sir," she protested, her expression confused.

"I assumed you hadn't heard the news as you've just

returned. That was a way to transition into it—call it subtle guiding." He turned his attention to her. "The Academy received a rather large contribution from the Mirai Corporation."

The ace glanced at his friend, whose eyes widened. "Mirai? What did they send?"

"A rather large contribution. I can't go into more details than that, but I can say that a board member fainted," he said dryly. "Along with it was a message stating that whatever funds necessary were to be set aside to pay for Chiyo Kana's contract." The commander took a tablet out and slid it across the table. "There is something personal for you as well."

Chiyo picked the tablet up, read it slowly, and placed a hand on her lips as tears began to form. She wiped them away quickly.

"Congratulations, Chiyo," Sasha said quietly. "And thank you to both of you for bringing this to our attention. You don't need to trouble yourselves with this anymore."

"Oh, you can't give us that treatment," Kaiden warned and stood abruptly. "We already decided that we'll take these guys on as well."

"Kaiden, this isn't a simple gig," the professor pleaded. "This could lead to—"

"A big war or something? Maybe, but you know what happens when I leave loose ends," he retorted. "I don't think they know we have all this info. We can strike before they have a chance to finish whatever they are trying to do."

"Even with this information, it will take a long while before we can take the proper measures," the commander explained. "For a thorough investigation, we may have to get the council involved."

"You can do whatever, but Chiyo and I have a copy of all that too," he said calmly.

She looked at the two staff members. "We are involved with this, sirs. We will deal with this one way or another."

Laurie looked at Sasha, who adjusted his oculars. "Determination makes a good soldier. It can also be rather annoying." He huffed his obvious frustration. "I can't stop you, especially as the two of you have no obligation to even remain here. However, if that is your decision—"

"It is," they replied in unison.

"Trust me, they have this on lock," Chief affirmed as he appeared beside Kaiden.

The commander smiled and placed a hand on Laurie's shoulder. "We will take care of things on our end. But until we can get everything in order, what can we do to help?"

Kaiden looked at Chiyo but she simply waited for his move and looked at him with assurance. "We have a general idea of where some of them are—or their facilities, at least," he said and fixed the two men with a firm look. "But I want to strike them somewhere that can't be easily fixed or replaced. Their main HQ would be nice, but we didn't find it in the files."

"Even if that isn't possible, something other than merely an automated facility like the one we found would work," she added.

"They would have a place like that well-guarded," Sasha pointed out. "Even all your friends together would have a hard time accomplishing something like that. And in this kind of situation, I would have to act as a board member and forbid—"

"I think that should be up to them," the ace stated. "But I have other associates if we can actually find them and put my plan into action."

"And what would that plan be, dear Kaiden?" Laurie asked.

He smiled and pounded his fist into his hand. "What I do best, obviously—a full-on assault."

ORIGIN STORIES

CHAPTER ONE

Chiyo Kana

"Is that her?" a woman in the hallway asked another as she tried to return to her desk with her beverage. "Orikasa san's daughter?"

"She's his ward, Makoto," her friend replied in another whisper, although they weren't far enough from earshot as she turned the corner, leaned against the wall, and retrieved her phone. "Orikasa san doesn't have any children by birth."

"Still, I had never seen her until now. I honestly thought it was only a rumor," Makoto replied. "I wonder what she is doing here. Do you think he brings her here to protect her? Maybe keep her out of public view?"

"I'm sure Sir Orikasa san has the funds to hire all kinds of caregivers and protection if he wanted to keep her at his house," her friend replied. "Perhaps he's training her to take over in the future."

"Do you really think so?" The woman frowned. "I don't

believe she would be accepted but the scandal is still somewhat fresh. I'm shocked that she simply walks around. She should understand that she is the cause of—" Her phone suddenly blared and a song echoed loudly along the corridor, the lyrics speaking of the small miseries of life—such as idle chatter.

"Why do you have your ringer on at work?" her friend demanded and stepped away hastily.

"It shouldn't be. I don't know this song." Makoto took her phone out frantically and peered at the screen. "No one is calling."

The young girl put her own phone away and sighed as she continued her walk to the security division. If he asked why she did that, she would say practice. He would know better, but that was only if he caught her.

"Nice try, Chiyo." Taro huffed as he took the canned coffee he'd asked her to get from her hand. "You know I have your devices scanned, right?"

She looked at the man with his shaved head and stern-looking eyes, yet they seemed rather relaxed at the moment and even bored. "You don't seem that annoyed," she stated and clambered onto a seat on the office chair opposite him in the tiny room.

"It's not like you tried to hack into the private servers again," he muttered and twisted the can open. "Randomly accessing another person's phone and causing a ruckus seems a little childish. Normal for a ten-year-old, of course, but that doesn't seem to be your style." He took a sip of his beverage and leaned back. His chair angled slightly as he rubbed his temples. "Although I'm not sure if my job would be easier or harder if you were a normal ten-year-old."

Chiyo shrugged and took small sips of her carbonated lychee drink. "I've seen other kids my age. My guess is that I would be bored." She looked curiously at him. "How could you tell what I was doing? I learned how to find and block signal emission even before I met you."

Taro rolled his eyes and placed his coffee on the table. "Do you really think I would have this job if I couldn't deal with something as simple as that, little one?"

She looked away and didn't reply.

The man shook his head. "I'll give you credit that when I looked at your device, nothing showed that you blocked my tracking program or hid your connection to the lady's phone. But I track everyone in this building. That woman's phone—Makoto? The settings changed way too quickly if she only used the application screen to implement them."

The girl frowned. "That sounds illegal."

He nodded. "Probably extremely so too, but if you want to be an effective hacker, you have to be fine with a little murkiness and potential jail time."

"What about white-hat hackers?" she asked.

He scoffed and reached for his can. "I said if you want to be an effective hacker, not a technically proficient janitor."

Her cheeks ballooned out in a show of annoyance. "I'm not sure you should be telling me this."

"Hey, the facts of life are tough on a kid," he admitted

with a self-assured smirk. "But you came to me, remember?"

"It was either that or you would tell my fa—Gendo I was looking into his files," she reminded him.

"I saw potential and still do, although your speed as a delivery girl could be quicker." He looked pointedly at the can. "This was almost at room temperature."

"I'll be sure to make it a priority next time," she responded sarcastically.

"Getting snippy now, huh?" He grinned. "Good. You need a little grit to do this right."

"You make quite a few assumptions," she retaliated and gestured around the room. "I'm not sure if my future involves all...this. You only seem to do odd jobs. How can that be fulfilling?"

Taro rolled his eyes again, a frequent habit in their discussions. "Man, you're so young and yet worried about job satisfaction. You need to loosen up, kid, and look to finding your own path." He drained the last of the coffee, crushed the can in his hand, and tossed it into a small recycle bin close to the door. "I do what I want. Have you any idea how hard to secure that kind of freedom in a big corporation like this is? I take care of the stuff that can't really be recorded for business reasons. Occasionally, I get big jobs. You've merely caught me in a slow period."

"Wasn't my case your last big job?" she inquired. "That seems to be rather silly—concerned over the crimes of a child."

"Not really. I was the same way," he admitted. "I was almost put in a juvenile prison for hacking into Mirai's servers seventeen years ago. I only wanted schematics I could blow up into posters. The man who had my gig back then discovered me and brought me in as an apprentice instead."

Chiyo tilted her head and regarded him with an expression that might have been understanding. "So this is full circle for you, then?"

"Maybe. It depends on whether or not you can get over your prepubescent life crisis."

She puffed her cheeks out in exasperation again and he chuckled. "You really need to stop with the obvious tells. It's not a good habit when you'll have to deal with actual people to obtain info. Besides, it makes you look like a long-haired pufferfish. You gotta have chill in this line of work." Taro looked up when the holoscreen behind her flashed. "It looks like something's finished—actually, the project I had you working on is finished."

The girl looked behind her and stretched her feet down to scoot the chair around to have a look. "It is. I've fixed all the problems in the simulation."

Taro smiled as he turned. "Good job. And that wasn't a simulation."

"What do you mean?" She stared at him, confused,

There was a knock on the door and the man called for whoever it was to enter. An older woman opened the door and a younger one with violet hair followed her in.

"Taro, Orikasa san wants to see— Why do you always have it so dark in here?"

"I get plenty of light from the monitor screen, Sayoko," he replied and twirled to face the older woman, although his attention was focused on her younger companion.

"Who's the new one who actually had the decency to bring color to the place?"

"This is Rei. She's my assistant," his visitor stated. "As for the color of her hair, she has already been made aware of company policy and should dye it back to its natural color soon, correct?"

Rei nodded meekly. Taro stood and motioned for Chiyo to follow. "You should keep it colorful. Despite all the design work we do here, the personnel lack expression."

"And you shouldn't abuse your power here," the woman muttered while she studied Chiyo. "Why are you taking her?"

"The boss wants to know how the progress on the system he asked me to verify is going, right?" he asked as the two of them left. "I should therefore bring the one who actually worked on it along."

Chiyo's eyes widened as the others walked down the hall. He looked back and beckoned for her to keep up. She took a deep breath and nodded before she rushed to his side.

Gendo stared silently at the two. Chiyo kept her head lowered but Taro had his hands in his pockets and leaned back lazily. He somehow seemed to look at the director and past him at the same time. "What do you think, boss? It's impressive, right?"

He looked at the screen again. "I see no problems. In

fact, I noticed a couple of issues that weren't reported were also fixed."

"She has a good eye for it," her mentor stated and placed a hand on the young girl's head. "I didn't even have to teach her all that much. She's at a level that something like this is basically normal schoolwork for her."

The director scrutinized his daughter. "I confess, I'm a little perturbed that you didn't consult with me before letting an unauthorized person—much less a child—look at one of our prototypes. However, I can't dispute that the work was completed thoroughly, and in good time as well." Chiyo looked up. His gaze was intense, but there was something else there beyond the normal unfathomable expression he normally displayed—something akin to interest and perhaps pride? No, she was altogether too hopeful.

Gendo turned to Taro. "She has remained in your office anytime I bring her here. I was worried she was in your way. This is what you have been working on?"

"I've worked on those other projects as well. You should receive the first run of Arsene tomorrow afternoon, by the way," he informed his boss. "Along with plugging some of the security risks the boys have missed."

The other man frowned and Taro stifled a chuckle. The internal security team would hear a few choice words soon.

"Very well, thank you for coming." The computer specialist bowed and Chiyo followed his lead. Without another word, they began to leave the office when the director called to her, "Chiyo,"

She spun and tried to keep her composure. "Yes, sir?"

"Good work," he said quietly before he returned to his work.

Her mentor patted her head as he opened the office door. The two stepped out and he closed it gingerly behind them. "I think that might have been the first time I heard him talk to you directly," he noted.

The girl nodded, looked down, and twisted her hands in her shirt.

"So…do you think you can see a reason why you should get better at this? I personally think it would be a waste of a gift to not—"

"I do," she mumbled. He noticed a couple of tears drop to the floor.

A little startled, he looked away and tried to think of something to lighten the mood. "Hey, Chi, I think I'm ready for lunch. Are you hungry? It's on me."

"That sounds nice," she responded and sniffled slightly as she wiped the tears quickly from her eyes.

"What do you feel like?"

"Do you like sushi?"

Taro grinned. "Sushi, huh? I only eat a few kinds, but there's a great conveyor place I like." He set off down the hallway with her close behind. "Sometime, I need to have you try takoyaki. It's these fried octopus balls. That stuff is fantastic."

She nodded. "Next time, when I finish the next project."

He glanced over his shoulder and grinned at the young girl. Her voice was still soft but now held a determination he hadn't heard previously. "That sounds good. I'll get you started when we get back."

CHAPTER TWO

"So we hope you will take it under consideration, Miss Kana," the man on the holoscreen said, his tone crisp and businesslike.

"I will. Although I doubt that will be sufficient for you. It hasn't been for any of the other Ark academy representatives who have contacted me." She sighed, her focus on the second screen where she passed easily through the practice server Taro had set up for her. If the actual security was this easy to bypass, they would all be in danger. Did they want to upgrade to this?

"It won't be any trouble. We are merely extending the offer," the rep explained. "Nexus Academy is always on the lookout for promising talent. Even in your more...secretive field. You show great promise and tremendous skill for a seventeen-year-old. There are people who have been in this field for as long as you've been alive and they don't match what we've seen. As an infiltrator myself, I can promise you will get the best education the world can offer."

"Infiltrator?" she questioned. "They are normally skilled in fighting as well, yes? I have some basic martial arts skills, but firearms are new to me."

"That's what the Animus is for," he explained. "Of course, there are other technician careers available. It may be a personal bias, but I believe the life of an infiltrator may be a more exciting change of pace. If you merely wanted to be a normal hacker, I doubt you'd gain any further significant knowledge that you don't already know."

"I would have to agree." She nodded and paused in her work for a moment to look at him. "Tell me something, Mister…"

"Raynor, but you can call me Ray if you like."

"Mr. Raynor, I never had the chance to ask the other representatives, but how exactly did you find me?"

He shrugged, a satisfied grin on his face. "I can't speak for the others, but I did say I was an infiltrator myself, right?"

"Several times now, yes." She nodded, "Still, I don't keep a record of myself here in Mirai. Nor does my…father, in any private capacity. So even if you or someone else were to find a way to hack into our systems without me noticing —which is quite unlikely, by the way—you would have found no record of me to peruse."

The man's eyes widened and he rubbed the back of his head a little awkwardly. "That's a fair point. I suppose it wouldn't be polite to withhold how we found out about you,"

"No need. I merely wanted to see your expression when confronted by that fact," she explained and stretched to turn the screen off. "I have my own suspects. I will consider your offer and if I wish to pursue it, I will call you once again."

"I…uh, see. Thanks for—" Chiyo deactivated the screen and cut him off. She took a moment to stretch before she leaned back in her chair and stared at nothing in particular. "There you are, my suspect," she stated when she noticed movement near the door. "It was you, wasn't it?"

"Whatever would give you that idea?" Taro asked, stepped out of the shadows, and handed her a plastic bag with a lidded bowl and utensils in it. "I got that miso ramen you asked for."

She nodded and smiled as she looked into the packet. "Over the past year, you have pushed me to look into other careers and I have shown no interest. My guess was that these academies received not only my information but examples of my accomplishments were also handed off by someone. The only one who has kept any kind of record or has enough knowledge on me to do so is you."

"Well now, that's an interesting idea," he conceded as he sat and opened a carton of takoyaki. "It would have to be someone you've worked extensively with. But I'm not the only teacher or partner you've had. It could have been Asuka, Tito, Ayane, Daidara—"

"They would know better," she interrupted, popped the lid off her bowl, and took the chopsticks from the bag. "I've surpassed them, anyway, so crossing me would be unwise."

"Crossing you, huh?" The man rolled his eyes. "I know I've drilled into you that you need to maintain chill to work as a hacker, but now, you're starting to sound like a supervillain."

"That's part of dealing with the murkiness, isn't it?" she replied and blew on the noodles to cool them before she ate several strands.

Taro set his carton aside and rubbed his temples. "All right, I'll give you the win because I know this kind of debate could go on for hours—"

"Where's your chill, Taro?" she asked with a hint of mirth.

"You seem to have a supernatural ability to sap it fairly quickly. It could be a useful skill. You should work on it," he retorted. "Come on, it's not a bad idea. Using the skills you have and applying them to a much more interesting profession? How could you go wrong?"

"What's wrong with wanting to stay here?" she inquired and deliberately made eye contact.

He sighed. "Chiyo, you're less than half my age and your skill is nearly almost on par with mine. I won't be able to teach you soon."

"We could still work together," she pointed out and a trace of concern finally revealed itself.

"For a while, but there's already talk to transfer me to another company of the zaibatsu."

"What?" Chiyo gasped, placed her bowl down quickly, and leaned forward. "That's foolish. I'm sure I could talk to father and—"

"Chiyo, if I leave, who do you think would take my place?" he asked. It didn't take long for the truth to dawn on her. "In fact, this transfer is only because he's recognized your talent. That should make you happy if that's all you're after."

She raised her knees to her chest. "Maybe at one point

that was what I wanted, but I've realized that he only sees me as another worker, skilled or not. There's nothing beyond it."

The man's gaze lowered and he shook his head. "He's not really a cuddler, is he? But I don't think..." She looked at him expectantly, but he waved her off. "It's not my place to guess. And before you say something smart, I'm not only doing this to save my cushy job. You have more drive than I ever did, Chiyo. It's something that took a while to really blossom, but I'm worried it will die if you stay here." He picked his carton up again and took a takoyaki. "You should be the heir of this whole company, but those assholes on the board won't allow that. Even if you got it, they would make your life miserable."

"That's simply how it is. My lineage is starting to make the rounds as gossip and I've even seen reports in foreign newsletters," she stated and avoided his gaze. "I have no reason to want the director's position anyway."

"If you had the opportunity, you might have a chance to actually think about it," he suggested and brandished the skewer as if to make his point. "It might merely be my own personal hang-up. I don't need to push it onto you."

Chiyo was silent for a moment before she smiled, "You were hoping I'd take over so your job would be even easier?"

"Silly dream, right?" he answered with a chuckle. "I don't know much about the whole infiltrator thing that guy went on about. It seems dangerous, but I think it's basically like a cyber assassin, right?"

"More akin to a thief, but I suppose a number of

hackers would be called that regardless," she explained. "It would be…different, certainly."

"So you'd be like a cyber fox?" Taro mused before he rubbed his head sheepishly. "That wasn't supposed to be a — Never mind."

"Don't worry yourself," she teased.

He leaned back and took another bite. "Like he said, you don't have to choose that class, but think about it, all right?"

"I actually have been," she said, uncrossed her legs, and stood. "I'll return soon."

"Where are you off to?"

"I need to report to the director."

———

"An Ark academy?" he asked curtly and stared at his daughter.

"Several have extended invitations," she replied calmly.

Gendo paused, stood, and walked past her to the windows, his usual place to think. "What are your plans?"

"That's what I'm here to determine."

He drew a deep breath and clasped his hands behind his back. "You aren't one to ask me for advice."

She shook her head. "I'm not here for advice, sir," she stated and the last word seemed to fall from her mouth like lead. "I wanted to know if this would cause complications for you."

"For me? No," he assured her. "There is always a place here for you, Chiyo, but you were never required to remain."

She wondered if required meant necessary. At least he had enough tact to replace the word if it did. She ran a hand up her arm. "I originally thought I would stay here and improve my craft, but I don't think I'll be able to improve much more by simply continuing to work on various small updates. I'll stagnate."

"That is true." He nodded "Someone of your skills could be very valuable and well-paid for their knowledge and ability. It would certainly enable you to create a path of your own."

A path. Taro had said things like that as well over the years.

"Do you think to begin freelance work after this education?"

"I...I do not know yet, but I don't think I'll focus only on hacking."

Gendo turned slightly toward her. "Ark academies train in a variety of skills. But the best one is easily Nexus Academy in America. Have they made you an offer?"

"They have."

He turned a little more. "And you know that they mostly focus on military, industry, and espionage, correct?"

"Of course, their representative made that clear," she confirmed.

"So when you say you won't focus on only hacking, I would have to surmise you would look into a field in which you can use your already acquired skills along with a new set. That could lead to any number of careers, but if you are seriously considering this, you'll go with your best option."

"That is correct."

Gendo stared at his daughter for a while before he nodded and turned away. After a moment, he withdrew a case from his pocket. "Take this."

She took it from him, a little confused. "What is it?"

"It is one of the Nexus EI chips. We've done work with them before and their lead researcher left me one as a gift. You should examine it to see if their tech meets your standards."

"I see." She looked at the case for a moment before she bowed as was expected. "Thank you. I'll inform you of my decision."

"Understood. Have a good evening." She accepted the dismissal and immediately turned and left him to return to his work. As soon as he sat, he sent a message to Taro.

We've talked. Thank you for sending the information.

He responded almost immediately. **Of course, boss. You spent all that time putting them together. I was surprised you kept such a thorough profile on her all these years. Plus, it wasn't like I wouldn't follow orders. You are the director.**

Gendo closed his eyes and rested his head back. He was the director, something he made sure everyone knew and something he took pride in. But every time he saw her, no matter how brief, he felt he had sacrificed something else to retain it.

Chiyo,
Thank you for your assistance in the matter of the attempted

espionage at Mirai. I wasn't aware that you would take action yourself. I haven't seen you since you began your second year. Even during the summer when you returned, you worked on your own projects. You have grown so much and you helped me immeasurably, even though there was no obligation to do so. I want you to know that without you around, I have taken the time to reflect that I should have done more while you were here. You are a gifted child and I tremble to think what would have happened if Taro did not see it. I would have let that spirit decay under my desire to pursue my own ideals. I want you to know that wherever your path takes you, I am more proud of you as a father than I ever was as merely a director.

I hope I can see you again.

Chiyo placed the tablet onto her dresser, sat on the bed in her dorm, and hugged herself, a smile on her lips as tears began anew. She had found her path, but there was so much farther to go.

CHAPTER THREE

Dario Adesso

Why had he returned? He wasn't satisfied. The assassin known to others only by the codename Umbra made a cursory study of the bunker. The last time he had been there was more than a year before. It held no special relevance for him. In fact, seeing the marks on the way in and the stains that had never been cleaned after the investigation, it sickened him more than anything. It had to. Otherwise, it would simply depress him.

His target at that time was a professional group of bounty hunters he had been sent to eliminate. He was one of their potential marks—not that day, obviously, but he would inevitably face them eventually and this way, he could also get paid.

14,470—that was the total amount needed to annihilate them. Granted, most of them fell in the initial blast, but those who recovered were still in able shape and should have lasted longer. Despite that, it was over and done within about nine minutes. He needed better targets. The sad truth was that he hadn't felt any real rush in years at this point. There was no longer a surprise strategy that forced him onto the defensive, no strong lone soldier who could drive him back, nothing at all gratifying in his work. Umbra tried to focus on the monetary pleasures his credits allowed him, but those wouldn't keep him satisfied much longer.

He peered at the message sent directly to him from an unknown source. It would have taken quite a few credits in and of itself—or extreme talent. The message told him to come to this location. He assumed it was from a group aligned with those bounty hunters who wanted revenge and wondered if they could be the challenge their peers were not. With the limitless patience of his particular craft, he stood in the center of the room. Moonlight seeped in through the cracks above and glimmered on the windows around him. He had deliberately given them the advantage in the fight, assuming they ever arrived.

"Dario Adesso?" a voice asked from somewhere ahead. Whoever spoke was obviously hiding in the shadows, but he was still mildly surprised. He hadn't heard anyone enter and hadn't seen anything on the scan. When did they arrive?

"You know my legal name, then?" he asked and his voice droned with bland annoyance as he folded his arms. "I suppose I'll have to change it again."

"That seems unnecessary," the voice replied. It was a calm but scholarly voice with a faint suggestion of obvious age but not someone advanced in years. Whoever this was, he was probably only a little older than himself.

"I don't believe anyone knows your night job other than myself."

"Is that right? You found out all on your lonesome, then?" Dario questioned and activated the night vision in his oculars. He could vaguely discern a shape in the darkness, but it was hazy. The stranger obviously used some kind of device of his own to tamper with tech.

"No, I am quite intelligent if I may compliment myself, but I am no skilled detective. I merely had the one I used to find you killed," the man explained. A light tapping along the ground was accompanied by footsteps. Dario straightened as a middle-aged man stepped into the moonlight, walking with a black cane with a silver handle. He had tanned skin and long dark hair and studied him with a glimmer in his eyes. "Good evening, my name is Merrick Rayne."

"Rayne?" he muttered and looked away in thought. "I thought I read about someone with that name who died recently."

"I am not someone who will let death hinder my plans. This world interests me more than any afterlife," the man said calmly.

Dario rolled his neck and sighed. "You can simply tell me you faked it. Fancy phrases and pretensions aren't really something I enjoy."

Merrick placed both hands on his cane. "And what do you enjoy, Mr. Adesso?"

"Not much, it seems—at least these days," he admitted and lowered his arms "I used to love a good fight, or maybe merely violence itself. But I can't find a thrill anymore. I came here hoping for a squad of revenge-hungry mercs to be waiting or something, but I assume you only want me to complete a gig for you?"

"Actually, I want you to join my organization." The unexpected statement caught him off guard. "You say your current occupation bores you? I can think of two reasons for that, maybe. One is purely a lack of good opponents. I can easily correct that."

"Is that right?" Dario demanded and settled his hands on his hips. "Since we're chatting and all, I'll hear number two."

"That would be the fact that there is no purpose behind why you fight," Merrick explained and pointed at him with his cane. "Under me, you'll have a reason. One that would not only give your work meaning but would also help this entire world find its place once more."

"The entire world…right…" Dario chuckled. "It sounds lofty and righteous—not really my thing. And under you? That isn't to my liking either."

"I thought fighters like yourself always recognized those stronger than them," Merrick countered, and his voice revealed neither satisfaction nor frustration.

He smirked as he turned away. "All right. I think I had better head off, now. You honestly seem like a rich guy with too much time."

"So the fact that I know who you are doesn't bother you, then?"

"I can't say that it does, *mio amico*. Like you said, I'm used to abandoning my name when it becomes inconvenient." He began to walk away with a casual and confident stride. "I'll let you live because I don't feel like making new nanos, even if it's only a few. Next time, try a merc group or something if you're only looking for warm bodies."

"I see. Then I suppose I'll have to convince you another way, Mr. Adesso." Dario shook his head and spun to catch the object he sensed had been thrown at him. He scowled at what appeared to be an ordinary throwing knife with no fancy metals or plasma lining. This guy was a—

He realized the man wasn't there. Where he had stood only seconds before was empty, although no footsteps suggested movement. For someone with a cane, he could move with surprising speed and agility. The assassin activated one of his gauntlets. He might as well humor him, perhaps leave a hole or three and see if he'd return for revenge sometime. It could be fun. However, as soon as his nanos began to spread, he received a warning of something above. He glanced up as his adversary dove toward him and drew a long blade from his cane. Dario's eyes widened and he scrambled back and formed a small energy shield with his nanos to block the blade. He stared in disbelief when the energy was cut through as if it were paper.

Merrick landed, held the blade up, and brandished it at the assassin. "That was a small shield, but it still takes about three hundred nanos to make, correct?"

He checked his nano count. His opponent was right—three hundred down—but the strike had merely cut the energy. At best, he should have lost only a third when the power dissipated.

"This is a dual-sided blade. One sends out an energy pulse that deactivates your particular model of nanos. The other side is a plasma blade," the man informed him. "That one is for you."

Dario held his other gauntlet up and activated it to release the other half of his nanos. For a brief moment, his heart raced and his lips twitched.

"If you won't take my offer as a contract assassin, I suppose I'll have to make you submit as a warrior." Merrick held the blade up and continued to stare a challenge. "I'll extend my offer once more, due to your reputation. Should you decline, I suppose I'll have no choice but to force you to accept, unless your reputation is all you have."

"What do you mean?" he asked while he formed spears behind him.

"If your skills don't impress me...well, I don't have the luxury of simply being able to change my name to have people forget about me. I have to be rid of them."

The assassin finally allowed a true smile to blossom rather than the indifferent smirks he had limited himself to for so long, "Thank God I found you."

CHAPTER FOUR

Their fight had begun ten minutes before and Dario was down to seventy thousand nanos. He had yet to so much as scratch Merrick's jacket. The man was fast—abnormally fast. While he didn't appear to wear armor, he could have an underlay with mods that allowed him to increase his speed and finesse. Or he could be a cyborg. That wasn't out of the question at this point.

But he had him now, he was sure of it. The longer their fight went on, the more he could spread his machines. The combatants weren't far apart, and to anyone with the right set of oculars, the two of them would appear to be in the eye of a hurricane of nanos. His plan was to keep his adversary in place and then cocoon him in the machines. It was a satisfying prospect, and there wouldn't even be a drop of blood left after the explosion.

The older man relaxed his stance and Dario raised an eyebrow. "Are you done already?"

"Are you disappointed?" he asked by way of reply. "I have to say I am as well. That is such an obvious ploy."

JOSHUA ANDERLE & MICHAEL ANDERLE

He clenched his teeth for a moment before his smirk slid into place. "So you can see them? Is this resignation to death I see?"

"I already said what it was," Merrick replied, slid a hand into his pocket, then withdrew it and held up what looked to be a bomb trigger. He opened the cap with a flick of the thumb and pressed the button down. "Disappointment."

Crazy bastard. The assassin immediately drew his nanos to him to form a barrier, but they didn't respond. Neither, he realized after a breath-holding moment, was there an explosion.

He glanced quickly at the other man who rolled the trigger in his palm as he said, "That set a bomb off, but not a traditional one—a virus."

When he pointed to the ceiling, Dario looked up and noticed a device with an antenna attached. He could barely make it out even though he looked directly at it.

"I've fought against people like you before. I merely needed time to confirm the proper sequence variation for your nanos," Merrick stated and flipped his blade to the plasma side. "I can't control them like you can, but they are on standby until I deactivate my device." He began to walk over to his adversary with the blade poised and ready. "I am quite disheartened, Dario. I had hoped it wouldn't be this easy to outwit you."

"Outwit?" he asked and held a hand up to draw his fingers back. "Is that what I'm doing as well?"

Two spears rocketed from behind the older man. He noticed barely in time to slice one in half but the other lacerated the side of his shoulder. As he grunted with pain, he flipped the blade again.

"That's a neat trick, isn't it?" the assassin boasted. "It's the same thing techs use when they develop nanotechnology—a type of electromagnetism they use to control small numbers of them at a time. I found a way to be able to use far more from longer distances. It's a pain in the ass to use, though—way too much shoulder movement and focus are required."

"I see." Merrick stood, his blade ready. "So you're not quite finished, are you?"

"Not at all." A crash from above drew his attention. The spear he had missed had pierced his device after he'd lost sight of it while they talked. The nanos were now back under his opponent's full control.

"I won't take any more chances, *capo*," Dario said mockingly and snapped a finger as dozens of bombs appeared to surround his target. "I'll make this swift—call it a thanks for showing me I can still have a good time." The bombs began to bundle around him, but he grasped the scabbard of his blade, pressed a button on the side, and thrust it into the ground. Electricity erupted from within in a dome that formed around him. It obliterated the closest bombs before it expanded rapidly and arced through the whole room. The assassin's eyes widened when he was caught in the blast and saw his nano count drop rapidly.

He forced himself to stay on his feet and fumbled to reach the canister on his hip. It should have been insulated from the blast, so he still had around ten thousand stored within. He froze when he realized he couldn't feel his arm. It occurred to him that it might have been from the shock, but when he tried the other, it felt strangely lighter. In that moment, pain screamed through him, the static gave way, and he sprawled painfully. Puddles of blood seeped beside him, and one of his gauntlets lay nearby with what remained of his arm still inside.

"If the truth be told, I am no extraordinary fighter, Dario," Merrick stated as he circled from behind him, replaced the blade in the deactivated scabbard, and knelt. "I knew how you fought, and I prepared accordingly. And yet you still managed to force me to use every trick I brought with me. That is impressive."

Dario, even without arms, was able to get to his knees and scowled at the bloody floor beneath him.

"So then, do you yield?" his adversary asked.

He chuckled. "One last thing—" He opened his mouth and a nanoblade protruded. Before the other man could react, he was able to slice into his face beside his left eye. He used the last of his strength to pounce and force the other man to the floor, hold the blade in his teeth, and thrust toward his throat. The attack stopped abruptly when the blade hidden under Merrick's wrist stabbed into his neck.

The blade fell from his mouth and he managed a shaky laugh. "Was that your last trick?" He slid sideways. "That's funny. I have no more either."

A low hum was the first thing to draw his attention—a ship engine by the sound of it. Dario opened his eyes groggily and stared at a circular frame with a green eye that simply looked at him. Asiton model? He pushed it out of the way and grimaced at a loud clang when his hand made contact.

His face contorted in shock when he realized his arms were now metallic.

"We can graft artificial skin onto it later." The assassin turned as Merrick approached with a cup of coffee. "Or perhaps you'd like to decorate it differently?"

"What happened?" he asked, pushed to a seated position, and fixed his gaze on the other man. "I thought you killed me."

"Not quite." Surprisingly, Dario was able to take and hold the proffered cup with his artificial limbs. He wondered if it was drugged or poisoned but shook the thought away. At this point, his host—for want of a better word because he had no idea how else to think of him—already had the chance to leave him for dead. It would be a really macabre joke to keep him alive merely to kill him with poison. "I brought this droid with me. It kept you alive long enough for us to bring you here where the others could do the rest."

He looked around and noticed several of the same droids floating about the room. "Those are Asitons, are they not?"

"They are, but no need to worry, however. They are quite tame."

Dario took a sip and appreciated the fact that the beverage was still piping hot. "I heard you say you're not much of a fighter. That has to be a lie."

"What makes you say that? Pride?" Merrick asked.

He shook his head, "Even with all your gadgets and tools, to use it in combat under constant pressure like you did? That's not the sign of some techie playing hero. You're trained."

"I am a former military and merc," he replied and placed a hand on his chest.

"Trust me, I know the difficulty in using fancy tech as your main weapon. Speaking of which, are my—"

The other man nodded. "I retrieved your gauntlets before taking off. All your armor and other tools are waiting in the bay. I can replace the nanos fairly quickly if you would like."

Dario put his cup down and rubbed the back of his head. The cold metal felt surprisingly welcome, although a part of him was still vaguely surprised that he seemed to be able to move his arms without thought. "Why do you want me? I'm sure a man like you could get hundreds of people to follow him for the creds."

"I already have that," Merrick stated surprisingly. "What I don't have is someone who can represent my passion."

"Represent your passion? What are you talking about?"

He grinned as he took a sip of his coffee. "Mr. Adesso, I have quite a lofty dream, as I've already hinted at, but part of realizing that dream means I cannot take the stage in a more deliberate or visible manner. I'll need someone who can, should that be necessary. I've actually watched you for some time."

"Since I eliminated those bounty hunters in that bunker we fought in," the assassin guessed.

"That's correct." The man nodded. "I had sent them to retrieve someone else, but when I saw you at work—equally graceful and destructive—I felt you were a much more interesting choice."

"I suppose I can agree with that." Dario chuckled. "So what is this dream, exactly?"

"I'm afraid I can't tell a mere acquaintance," Merrick stated and took another sip before he put his cup down. "You don't work for me, I simply did this in gratitude for a good fight. You're free to leave if you wish."

The assassin looked from the man to his new artificial limbs. "Just like that? You'll even leave the arms?"

"I certainly have no use for them," he confirmed. "Do as you like."

Dario pushed from the medical bed, stretched, and made a few more complex motions to confirm that he was, in fact, already accustomed to his new arms. "Do you still want me?"

Merrick tilted his head, "The real question is, do you acknowledge me?"

Dario looked at him with a wide, feral smile, "I think I may even respect you a little."

"Is that so?"

He turned to point at the older man. "That doesn't mean I won't challenge you again. I still have my pride which demands satisfaction."

"Of course. You seem capable of that. If you finish your assignments with time to spare, I will take the time for whatever you wish," he stated and held a hand out. "Deal?"

Dario nodded and took the hand in a forceful hold, but his companion didn't even wince. "That's a deal, *capo*."

CHAPTER FIVE

Sasha Chevalier

"This is your last mission, isn't it, Commander?"

"Hmm?" Sasha turned to the soldier behind him on the dropship. "Oh...yes, I'll transfer to the Nexus Academy next month."

This drew a few snickers from the group of ten soldiers. Some leaned over to check a tablet. Bets had obviously been placed. What they might be, the commander didn't know, but it was probably at his expense.

"I can't tell if I'm more worried about you or the kids you'll take care of," Lieutenant Ren mused. "You complain about us all the time. Do you really think you'll have more peace at a place full of teens and twenty-somethings?"

"Are you saying the same about our ensigns, lieutenant?" he inquired. Ren glanced around sheepishly at the eight ensigns who regarded her angrily.

"Hey, don't scare him off," Ensign Calloway whispered loudly. "You'll lose the promotion that way."

JOSHUA ANDERLE & MICHAEL ANDERLE

"That ain't how it works, Ensign," Lieutenant DeMarco said and shook his head before he focused on the commander. "You'll finally be back on Earth, then? It's been ages for you, hasn't it?"

Sasha adjusted his rifle and slung it across his shoulder as he took his helmet in his hands. "That's normal for those of us in the navy, is it not?"

"We're in space plenty, but we still make time to get back to ground for leave," Ren pointed out. "You always hang around the embassy or some other station. Not to pry, sir, but I don't think I'll have another chance to ask if there was something holding you back."

"I can't simply enjoy space more?" he asked calmly as he pulled his helmet on.

DeMarco turned his comms on. "I guess that's possible, but I've seen you staring down from the window in that bar you like. That's the look of someone who misses something."

The commander looked at him with amusement. "I wish you were this perceptive when trying to deduce if I wish to be alone or not, Lieutenant."

"I am, but that would basically be anytime we're not on a mission." He chuckled and glanced at the door. "Speaking of which, do we have visual on the station yet? I hear this is supposed to be—"

"Ladies and gents, prepare yourselves," the pilot warned over the intercom. "Things have not lightened up since we departed so we're going in hot."

"God, the silence of space is morbid." DeMarco sighed and readied his cannon. "There's a full-blown battle going on and I don't hear a thing."

Sasha took the tablet and activated it to display a hologram of the station. "Queen, we'll go into one of the hangars, correct?"

"That's correct, sir. Hangar four seems to be the safest option. But I assume you're about to make a suggestion that's less so?"

"There should be a large enough access port that we can fly into, which will drop us off in the middle of the station," he explained. "It would put us within only a few kilometers of our retrieval target."

"Or I can use one of the massive holes that have already been blown into the station," she noted with a hint of concern.

Sasha pursed his lips. "How is the battle going?"

"There aren't enough forces close by for this to be a real battle, sir. The pirates have the upper hand. Any battleships here are simply to clear a path and make time for all the teams to retrieve hostages and objects of importance. I'm not sure when they'll pull back."

"We should have thirty minutes at least," Ren suggested.

"We should be out in ten. Queen will have to stay in flight to defend herself and there are enemy fighters still around," the commander pointed out.

"Don't worry about me, Commander. I'll make sure all the kids get back home," she promised.

"Are everyone's weapons at the ready?" he asked and all soldiers immediately confirmed this. "Queen, when we get inside the station and we have oxygen and gravity, unlock the doors and we'll lay down cover fire until you can find a place to slow enough for us to jump."

"The oxygen is no issue but the gravity is, sir," she

stated. "It looks like the artificial gravity field in that section is out."

He opened the chamber of his sniper rifle, removed the kinetic core, and replaced it with an energy core. "Only in that section or the whole station?"

"Right now, only in section B and F. Your target is in D and both C and D have gravity."

"That will be fine. When we're near a bridge, bank to the left and open the door. We'll use the mag boots," Sasha stated and looked at his team. "Lieutenant Ren and Ensign Calloway, you're with me. We'll eliminate any immediate targets when we're in the air while the rest of the team makes it to the ground. All of you, be careful. Mag boots will help to keep you in place but your range of motion and speed will be reduced."

"I didn't plan to run anywhere except towards the target, sir," Ensign Tucker stated cheerfully.

"Good boast, kid," DeMarco complimented him and pressed a switch on his cannon. "But don't get too cocky."

The ship began to nosedive and they adjusted to maintain their balance. "Heading into the port now, Commander."

Sasha stood and held onto the railing in front of the door with his rifle at the ready. He allowed himself one last look at his team, who had now lined up behind him. "You have your orders," he said crisply, turned away, and held his weapon in both hands. "Let's get this done and celebrate."

"The door will open in five…four…three…" He braced himself as the light on the lock changed from red to white before the door opened and he plunged out. The lack of gravity almost made him spiral but that was the plan. It allowed him to quickly scan the area and his trained eye identified almost a dozen enemies, although they seemed more distracted by the remaining security bots than the new group in their midst. It wouldn't remain that way for long, though.

Ren and Calloway followed, both with their rifles ready. The trio found their rhythm, located their targets, and eliminated them systematically. The energy blasts had much less kickback than kinetic rounds, but they were still tossed around somewhat. The continual motion made finding new targets easier, however, and each of them faced away from one another for the most effective distribution of fire.

The main group was able to pull themselves to the ground with hooks. They landed and DeMarco immediately delivered a series of rapid volleys at anything in the pirates' red and black colors. He made no effort to avoid the security bots in the way.

"Sir, I've found a route that will take us to Section C," Ensign Kali informed him over the comms.

"Understood, good work," Sasha stated and fired one more shot at a desperate pirate who tried to swoop toward him while his back was turned. He removed the hook shot from his belt and fired it at the bridge. "Ren, Calloway, we'll join with the others. When we have gravity again, switch to kinetic rounds."

"Understood, sir," Ren stated as he and Calloway followed his lead, fired hooks to the bridge, and reeled themselves in. They activated their mag boots once they landed.

The commander, after checking for any immediate threats, walked up behind DeMarco, who was busy lasering through one of the doors. "Thanks to the lack of gravity, we'll get through the next hall in no time and soon be in section C," the man informed him."But once we get there, it'll be a little more tricky. There are still numerous pirates, and my guess is that means there are fewer security droids for backup."

"Be glad they haven't hacked any yet," Sasha stated and while his subordinate finished his task, he stepped up to the rest of the team. "Kali, have you mapped a path?"

"Yes, sir." She nodded and showed him a hologram of the station. "The one you proposed is still mostly solid, but there was a breach here on the upper level of D."

"Dammit. That didn't compromise the target did it?" Sasha asked.

"No, sir. The beacon is still active, but it looks like they moved to this room here." Kali enlarged the area under discussion and traced a finger down the hall. "Once we get into C from this point, we can go up two floors and make our way into this section from the door. It's most likely reinforced due to security measures."

"I won't be able to hack in very quickly without the proper codes," Ensign Cavazos noted. "And getting them remotely without being shot or alerting any potential pirates still looking into the system will be a problem."

"Not to worry," DeMarco boasted while he patted his cannon. "Get me to the door and give me five minutes."

"If that doesn't suffice, we'll use explosives," the commander decided and shortened the barrel of his rifle. "This might take a little longer now—fifteen minutes, at most. Queen will rendezvous at the nearest hangar." He vented his rifle and nodded at his team. "We have a hostage to save. Let's get this done."

"Yes, sir!" they all replied and DeMarco kicked the door in as they proceeded into the next chamber.

CHAPTER SIX

"How's that door coming, Lieutenant?" Sasha asked and peeked around the corner once more.

"The damn thing is resilient!" the other man muttered at almost the halfway point.

"What happened to all that boasting, DeMarco?" Ren teased from where she studied the hologram with Kali and Cavazos.

"I drained too much energy saving your ass from the pirate in the mech," he countered. "Where's the thank you for that, by the way?"

"Waiting at a bar somewhere," she replied and her breath hitched. "Dammit, sir, we have a problem."

"What's wrong?" the commander asked and approached the hologram on which a section now blinked an angry red. "Hostiles?"

She nodded. "They seem to be coming in from the levels below. There's a gate in their way, but if they've been able to run around this easily, I'll bet that they have the means to break through."

"I agree." He nodded and looked at the door. "DeMarco, make a few swipes at the bottom of the door, then use explosives to force your way in, retrieve the hostage, and get to the hangar."

"Right, sir," he yelled before he released the trigger of his cannon. "Wait—where are you going?"

"To take care of the intruders," Sasha stated calmly and headed off without another word.

"Sir, wait!" Ren called after him. "It's not merely a team or a small group. There are at least twenty-five life signs coming this way, and we don't know what they are equipped with."

"I'll manage." He checked his ammo. "I'll find another exit where Queen can pick me up, but the hostage is priority."

She stepped beside him and hefted her rifle. "I'll go with you."

"Are you ready for that promotion, Lieutenant?"

"From this point on, it's a straight route to the hangar when they retrieve the hostage. If they need sniper support, they have Calloway," she pointed out. "Your plan is to buy time so they don't potentially catch up to us and flank us from the rear, right? The faster we eliminate them, the easier we can make things for everyone. I can even assist to find an extraction point."

Sasha looked from her to the others, who were busy placing explosives against the door. "DeMarco!" he called and the demolitionist looked at him. "You have command until we meet up. Finish this safely, all right?"

The man nodded and gave him a thumbs-up with his large gauntlet. "Of course, Commander. See you in ten."

"Maybe we should stop trying to guess the time at this point," Sasha admitted as he and Ren made their way down to intercept the pirates.

"Do you think it's a bomb or laser?" Ren asked as they perched on a railway above the room, their rifles aimed at the door.

"They could simply have the access codes by now," he replied and adjusted his scope. "Either way, take out as many as you can while they're still in disarray, then make sure to keep on the move when they retaliate."

"Understood. I have my EI looking for an exit. So far, our best bet is actually through the doors."

"The hangar is three kilometers from there," Sasha pointed out.

"There's a breach to the left. You have a small oxygen tank, right? We can jump from the breach and have Queen scoop us up."

"That seems risky. If it comes to that, we need to notify the team to activate their own— Wait, here they come."

The doors opened without any explosion or laser fire and a well-built man in his late twenties with a coarse beard and shaved head walked in. He was shirtless and carried a shotgun, "Captain's dead, huh?" he asked one of the pirates beside him.

"Yeah. Lokean is next in line."

The man smirked, took a cigarette out, and placed in his mouth. He swiped a match across his cheek to light it. "Not after I get through with him." He chuckled and blew out a slow trail of smoke. "Now, where are these fancy soldiers you were fretting about?"

"That's Swarn," Ren told her superior. "He's one of the top ranks in the Dead Space Pirates."

"Let's take him, Ren—" Sasha pushed her away as a blast rocked their railway and almost toppled it.

"Never mind, I found them." The invader smiled. "We have you on camera, idiots. None of that sneaky stuff now."

The commander braced himself against the railing, fired four shots in rapid succession, and felled four of the pirates. The remainder scattered.

Ren vaulted to another railway, spun, and fired two shots to eliminate two of the enemy who had yet to reach cover. But to prove that didn't matter, she shot a third through the machine the others used as a shield. The wounded man sagged, and the bullet sparked against another piece of metal and caused the machine to explode and obliterate his comrade.

Sasha allowed himself to drop from his elevated position. He continued to fire through his descent and delivered a few fatal strikes before the enemy began to return fire. His stealth generator activated with a swift press of a button before he landed and sprinted across the floor. The invaders fired wildly and he had to dodge the fusillade while he reloaded. A shock grenade soared overhead and a pirate tried to catch it to throw it back, but his grasp slipped and it erupted to shock both him and his partner.

Where had Swarn gone? He'd had him in his sights as he fell, but once he landed, the man had vanished. Did he run and leave his grunts to clean the mess up? His thoughts were rattled from his head when something chopped against his neck. He was flipped before he could retaliate, and his rifle slid from his hands as he landed hard. The force of the impact shattered his generator and he was instantly visible.

"Like I said, no sneaky stuff," Swarn mocked. He now wore a red monocle of some kind that must have enabled him to see beyond the stealth shield. The pirate aimed his shotgun directly at Sasha's chest and his finger tightened on the trigger.

Ren plummeted from above and drove a blade into his shoulder. He cursed as he spun, caught her by the back of her helmet, and hurled her into the wall. Before she could recover from the painful collision, he walked up and pounded his boot into her stomach. The remaining pirates made their way over quickly with their weapons ready.

"That hurt like hell, missy," the leader growled and now focused on her as he prepared to fire. "But I'm a gentleman. I'll make this quick."

The commander activated a thermal and rolled it along the floor as he drew his own blade. "Shit! Grenade!" One of them yelled a warning and the man spun to see what was happening. His momentary distraction allowed Sasha to vault up and thrust his blade through the pirate leader's left eye. Swarn hissed and attempted to punch his attacker, who dodged easily and responded with a downward slash directly beside the original wound. The invader howled with rage and began to fire at random while he held the eye with his free hand. Ren kicked savagely and toppled him as the grenade behind them detonated. Sasha's shields burst and the back of his armor cracked, but he and Ren raced through the room to the entrance. They took turns to twist and fire behind them with their pistols as they made their escape.

"Are you all right, Ren?" he asked and killed one of the pursuing pirates with two shots to the chest.

"I should ask you that," she muttered and held her stomach. "We should have finished that brute."

"Another time. Perhaps that could be your first mission," he suggested and noticed a turn a little farther down the hall. "This way."

"We're going with my plan?" she asked.

"We don't currently have much choice," he admitted and fired a few shots blindly behind him before he dropped his remaining thermal as they turned the corner. The blast erupted and he activated the comms. "DeMarco, what's your status?"

"I was about to call you. Sir. We're on the dropship with the package. Where are you?"

"Track our location. We'll have to make our escape through a breach."

"Really? That sounds too cool to be your idea, sir," the man said jokingly.

"It was Ren's. But be ready. We have hostiles in pursuit."

"Not to mention the fighters around here. We're on our way." DeMarco signed off as the two rounded another corner. Gravity vanished almost instantly and they used the walls and scaffolding to push off to quicken their escape. They found the breach in the station's side and Sasha's oxygen meter appeared as they approached. Ren pushed off the wall and drifted through the opening and out into open space with him a short distance behind.

The dropship drew closer. When he felt something snag

his belt, he looked down to see Ren had tied them together. She adjusted her rifle and aimed away from the ship, and he realized she still had kinetic rounds. A single shot was all they needed to provide a surge forward and bring them beside the ship. The door opened and DeMarco and Calloway reached out to help them in. An enemy fighter banked and turned toward the vessel.

Sasha thumped the button to close the door. "Punch it!"

The ship rocketed forward as the fighter attempted to close in. The soldiers braced against the sudden boost. DeMarco held the hostage—a lead researcher—in place as they surged clear. The other dropships in the area were already leaving and the battleships slowly pulled out after them. It was over.

"A farewell to our dear commander," DeMarco shouted as the team raised their glasses in a toast. They began to chat excitedly to each other, to congratulate Ren on her upcoming promotion, and say their goodbyes to Sasha. He excused himself from the others a little later and wandered over to a window to look out at his home planet below.

"You really do miss it, don't you?" Ren asked as she walked up behind him.

"I'm sure that in time, I'll grow sick of it. That's what led me here in the first place." He smiled and finished his whiskey.

"You never gave a straight answer on why you took that teaching job," she commented and leaned against the wall. "I know it's your alma mater and everything, but do you really think you can be— Wait, never mind. I guess you've taught me more than enough to qualify as a teacher."

"You were a fast learner as well, Ren," he pointed out. "You'll surpass me quite quickly, I imagine."

"You would be a captain now if you hadn't already taken the job," she reminded him and swirled the liquid in her glass. "I wanted to thank you for recommending me."

"It was earned, Meili," Sasha said with a firm look at his lieutenant. "Don't forget that."

"I won't," she promised and stared at Earth with him. "So why did you take it?"

Sasha was silent for a moment, and she assumed he would simply leave it unanswered. Instead, he took in a deep breath and said, "You'll see many soldiers in your life and probably have already. You see such potential in them. Some don't realize it while they are alive. If I can help them realize it early on and guide them, I'll worry less about whether there was more I could do."

Ren shifted slightly. "Wow, that's…" She took a sip and rolled it in her mouth before she swallowed. "That's quite deep."

"Laurie would consider it overdramatic, perhaps." He chuckled.

She squeezed her index finger and thumb together. "Just a little." Hollering from the table demanded their presence. "It looks like the party's still going and it's your last time with us all together. Wanna come?"

Sasha took one last look at the planet and nodded as she returned to the festivities. He hoped he could form new relationships there that were as meaningful as these.

Kaiden and friends are now available in audio at Amazon, Audible and iTunes. Check out book one, INITIATE, performed by Scott Aiello.

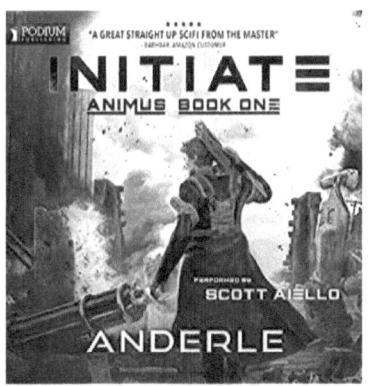

Check out book one at Amazon

(Book two is also available in audio, with more coming soon.)

AUTHOR NOTES - MICHAEL

JUNE 16, 2019

THANK YOU for not only reading this story but these *Author Notes* as well.

(I think I've been good with always opening with "thank you." If not, I need to edit the other *Author Notes*!)

RANDOM (*sometimes*) THOUGHTS?

What do you do when you haven't known your talent for forty-seven years?

You find out that you are grateful you found it eventually.

I didn't write and finish a book until 2015. Once I completed my first, I wrote two more (both over 60,000 words) in the next thirty days.

Then another in about three weeks.

Eventually, fans found my stories, and the rest is an amazing journey that still confuses me (in a good way) three and a half years later.

So much has changed in my world, and I owe it all to readers. Readers who read my books, my collaborators' books, and those of authors from around the world I've never heard of, and yet we all simply desire to write a story others enjoy.

As a reader, I felt like the one receiving the gift, and never knew what it felt like to share my art and have others (readers) talk to me about how it made them feel.

If you read a story that moves you (to tears, to laughter, to joy, to anything that matters to you) remember that somewhere there is an author who appreciates you taking your time to read.

I sure do.

AROUND THE WORLD IN 80 DAYS

One of the interesting (at least to me) aspects of my life is the ability to work from anywhere and at any time. In the future, I hope to re-read my own *Author Notes* and remember my life as a diary entry.

Cave in the Sky(™) Las Vegas, Nevada

I had dinner this evening with my wife Judith, Mike Bray from Wolfpack Publishing, and Mark Abbot from Publisher's Weekly. We ate Italian at Battista's Hole in the Wall and enjoyed ourselves.

I'm fifty-one now. I'm officially in the "older fart" category because I simply enjoyed sitting there and talking.

I'm an introvert. Sitting and talking isn't one of the top items on my list of fun things to do with other people.

Yet, we did.

I think I will enjoy this stage of my life.

FAN PRICING

$0.99 Saturdays (new LMBPN stuff) and $0.99

Wednesday (both LMBPN books and friends of LMBPN books.) Get great stuff from us and others at tantalizing prices.

Go ahead. I bet you can't read just one.

Sign up here: http://lmbpn.com/email/.

HOW TO MARKET FOR BOOKS YOU LOVE

Review them so others have your thoughts, and tell friends and the dogs of your enemies (because who wants to talk to enemies?) *Enough said ;-)*

Ad Aeternitatem,

Michael Anderle

CONNECT WITH THE AUTHORS

Michael Anderle Social
   Website:
   http://lmbpn.com

Email List:
   http://lmbpn.com/email/

Facebook Here:
   https://www.facebook.com/OriceranUniverse/
   https://www.
facebook.com/TheKurtherianGambitBooks/
   https://www.facebook.com/groups/
320172985053521/ (Protected by the Damned Facebook
Group)

www.ingramcontent.com/pod-product-compliance
Lightning Source LLC
Chambersburg PA
CBHW031621100726
47898CB00006B/1888